Abby Green got hooked on Mills & Boon® romances while still in her teens, when she stumbled across one belonging to her grandmother in the west of Ireland. After many years of reading them voraciously, she sat down one day and gave it a go herself. Happily, after a few failed attempts, Mills & Boon bought her first manuscript.

Abby works freelance in the film and TV industry, but thankfully the four a.m. starts and the stresses of dealing with recalcitrant actors are becoming more and more infrequent, leaving more time to write!

She loves to hear from readers, and you can contact her through her website at www.abby-green.com. She lives and works in Dublin.

MISTRESS TO THE MERCILESS MILLIONAIRE

BY
ABBY GREEN

™ MILLS & BOON®

First published in Great Britain 2009
Harlequin Mills & Boon Limited,
Eton House, 18-24 Paradise Road, Richmond, Surrey TW9 1SR

© Abby Green 2009

ISBN: 978 0 263 87439 6

Set in Times Roman 10¼ on 12 pt
01-1009-58867

Harlequin Mills & Boon policy is to use papers that are natural, renewable and recyclable products and made from wood grown in sustainable forests. The logging and manufacturing process conform to the legal environmental regulations of the country of origin.

Printed and bound in Spain
by Litografia Rosés, S.A., Barcelona

MISTRESS TO THE MERCILESS MILLIONAIRE

This is for Lorna Mugan and Anne Warter,
whose friendship I value so much.

PROLOGUE

KATE LANCASTER stood at the very ornate stone font where her two-month-old goddaughter was being christened. The holy water was being poured onto her forehead as the priest said a blessing in French. The ceremony was achingly beautiful, in a tiny ancient chapel in the grounds of her best friend Sorcha's new home, a stunning château just outside Paris. Kate had been at her wedding in this same chapel just nine months previously, as maid of honour.

And yet this moment in which Kate wanted nothing more than to focus fully on the christening was being upstaged effortlessly by the tall man who stood to her right. *Tiarnan Quinn.*

He'd also been at the wedding, as best man; he was Sorcha's older brother.

Kate tried to stem the pain, hating that it could rise here and taint this beautiful occasion, but she couldn't stop it. He was the man who had crushed her innocent ideals, hopes and dreams. The man who had shown her a moment of explosive sensuality and in the process ruined her for all other men. And yet she knew she had no one to blame but herself. If she hadn't been so determined to— She ruthlessly crushed that line of thinking. It was so long ago she couldn't believe it still affected her. That it still felt so fresh.

Despite her best efforts to block him out she could feel the heat from his large body envelop her, his scent wind around her, threatening to burst open a veritable Pandora's Box of memories. The familiar weight of desire she felt whenever she was near him lay heavy within her, a pooling of heat in her belly, between her legs. Usually she was so careful to avoid him, but she couldn't here—now. Not at this intimate ceremony where they were being made godparents in this traditional ritual.

She'd survived the wedding; she'd survive this. And then walk away and hope that one day he wouldn't affect her so much. But how long had she been hoping for that now? A sense of futility washed through her—especially as she recognised that if anything her awareness of him was growing exponentially stronger.

Her jaw was tight from holding it so rigid, her back as straight as a dancer's. She tried to focus on Sorcha and Romain. They were oblivious to all except themselves and their baby. Romain took Molly tenderly from the priest, cradling her easily with big hands. He and Sorcha looked at one another over their daughter's head, and that look nearly undid Kate completely. It was so private; so full of love and hope and earthy sensuality, that it felt voyeuristic to be witnessing it. And yet Kate couldn't look away or stop her heart clenching with a bittersweet pain, momentarily and shamingly jealous of what they shared.

This was what Kate wanted. This was all she'd ever wanted. A fulfilment that was so simple and yet so rare. Tiarnan shifted beside her, his arm brushing against hers, making her tense even more rigidly. Against her will she looked up at him; she couldn't *not*. He'd always drawn her eyes to him, like a helpless moth to the certain death of a burning flame.

He was looking down at her and her heart stopped, breath faltered. He frowned slightly, an assessing look in his gaze as he seemed to search deep within her soul for her secrets. He'd looked at her like that at the wedding, and it had taken all her strength to appear cool. He was looking at her as if trying to figure something out. Figure *her* out. Kate was so raw in that moment—too raw after witnessing Romain and Sorcha's sheer happiness and love. It was worse than the wedding. She had no defence here with a tiny baby involved—a tiny baby she'd held in her arms only a few moments ago. Holding that baby had called to the deepest, most primitive part of her.

Normally she coped so well, but with Tiarnan looking at her so intently her protective wall of icy defence was deserting her spectacularly, leaving in its place nothing but heat. And she couldn't do anything to stop it. Her eyes dropped betrayingly to his mouth. She quite literally yearned to have him kiss her, hold her. *Love her.* Look at her the way Romain had just looked at Sorcha. She'd never wanted that from any other man, and the realisation was stark now, cutting through her.

Against her volition her eyes rose to meet his again. *He was still looking at her.* Despite everything, she knew the futility of her secret desires; the feelings within her were rising like a tidal wave and she was helpless to disguise them, caught by the look in his eyes. She also knew, without being able to stop it, that he was reading every raw and naked emotion on her face, in her eyes. And as she watched his blue eyes darkened to a glittering shade of deep sapphire with something so carnal and hot that she instinctively put out a hand to search for something to cling onto, seriously fearful that her legs wouldn't support her.

He'd never looked at her with such explicit intensity…it had to be her imagination. It was all too much—and here she was, pathetically projecting her own desires onto him…

It was only after a few seconds that she realised Tiarnan had clasped her arm with a big hand. He was holding her upright, supporting her… And right then Kate knew that all her flimsy attempts to defend herself against him for years were for naught. He'd just seen through it all in an instant. Seen through *her.* Her humiliation was now complete.

CHAPTER ONE

One month later. Four Seasons Hotel, downtown San Francisco

KATE felt even more like a piece of meat than usual, yet she clamped down on her churlish thoughts and pasted on her best professional smile as the bidding continued. The smack of the gavel beside her made her flinch minutely. The fact that the gavel was being wielded by a well-known A-list Hollywood actor was not making the experience any easier. Despite her years of experience as a top model, she was still acutely uncomfortable under scrutiny, but she had learnt to disguise it well.

'Twenty-five thousand. Twenty-five thousand dollars to the gentleman here in the front. Am I bid any higher?'

Kate held her breath. The man under the spotlight with the unctuous grin was a well-known Greek shipping magnate. He was old, short, fat and bald, and his beady obsidian eyes were devouring Kate as he practically licked his lips. For a second she felt intensely vulnerable and alone, standing here under the lights. A shudder went through her. If someone else didn't—

'Ah! We've a bidder in the back—thirty thousand dollars from the new arrival.'

A rush of relief flooded Kate and she tried to strain to see past the glaring spotlights to identify who the new bidder was. It appeared as if the ballroom lighting technicians were trying to find him too, with the spotlight lurching from coiffed person to coiffed person, all of whom laughed and waved it away. The bidder seemed determined to remain anonymous. Well, Kate comforted herself, whoever it was couldn't be any worse a prospect to kiss in front of all these people than Stavros Stephanides.

'And now Mr Stephanides here in the front is bidding *forty* thousand dollars…things are getting interesting! Come on, folks, let's see how deep your pockets are. How can you turn down a chance to kiss this lovely lady *and* donate generously to charity?'

Kate's stomach fell again at Stephanides' obvious determination—but then the actor spied movement in the shadows at the back. '*Fifty* thousand dollars to the mysterious new bidder. Sir, won't you come forward and reveal yourself?'

No one came forward, though, and inexplicably the hairs rose on the back of Kate's neck. Then she saw the look of almost comic indignation on Stephanides' face as he swivelled around to see who his competitor was. The Greek's expression visibly darkened when someone leant low to speak in his ear. He'd obviously just been informed as to the identity of the mysterious fellow bidder. With an audible splutter Stephanides upped the ante by raising the bidding in a leap to one hundred thousand dollars. Kate held in her gasp at the extortionate amount, but her smile was faltering.

She became aware of the ripple of hushed whispers and a distinct frisson of excitement coming from the back; whoever this person was, he was creating quite a buzz. And then whoever it was also calmly raised their bid—to a cool two hundred thousand dollars. It didn't look as if her ordeal was going to end anytime soon.

Tiarnan Quinn wasn't used to grand, showy gestures. His very name was the epitome of discretion. Discretion in everything: his wealth; his work; his life, and most definitely in his affairs. He had a ten-year-old daughter. He didn't live like a monk, but neither did he parade his carefully selected lovers through the tabloids in the manner so beloved of other men in his position: a divorced heterosexual multi-billionaire male in the prime of his life.

None of his lovers had ever kissed and told. He made sure that any ex-partner was so well compensated she would never feel the need to break his trust. He always got out before any messy confrontations, and he always kept his private life very private. None of his lovers ever met his daughter because he had no intention of marrying ever again, and to introduce them to Rosalie would be to invite a level of intimacy that was reserved solely for his family: his daughter, sister and mother.

His lovers provided him with relief. Nothing more, nothing less.

And yet here he was now, bidding publicly, albeit discreetly for the moment, in the name of charity, for a kiss with Kate Lancaster—one of the most photographed women in the world. Because something in his mind and body was chafing, and for the first time in a long time he was thinking discretion be damned. He wanted this woman with a hunger he'd denied for too long. A hunger he'd only recently given himself permission fully to acknowledge and to believe it could be sated.

And it had been a long time building—*years*. He could see now that it had been building with a stealthy insidiousness into a subconscious need that was now very conscious—a burning necessity. His mouth twisted; those years hadn't exactly been uneventful or allowed much time for contemplation. A short-lived marriage and an acrimonious divorce, not to mention becoming a single parent, had taken up a large part of that time. If he'd had the luxury of time on his hands he might have realised a lot sooner— He halted his thoughts. No matter. He was here now.

His attention came back to Kate, focused on Kate, and he had the uncanny sensation of being in the right place at the right time. It was a sensation he usually associated with business, not something more emotional. He corrected himself; this wasn't about emotion. It was desire. Unfulfilled desire.

Perhaps it was because he'd finally allowed himself to think of it again—that moment ten years ago—but it was as if the floodgates had opened on a dam. It had been little more than a kiss, and yet it was engraved more hotly onto his memory than anything he'd experienced before or after. It had taken all of his will-power and restraint to pull away from her that night. Since then Kate had been strictly off-limits to him for myriad reasons: because that incendiary moment had shaken him up a lot more than he cared to admit; because she'd been so young *and* his little sister's best friend.

He remembered the way her startlingly blue eyes had stared directly into his, as if she'd been able to see all the way into his soul. As if she'd wanted him to see all the way into hers. *She'd looked at him like that again only a few weeks ago.* And it had taken huge restraint for him to allow Kate to retreat back into her shell, to ignore his intense desire. Until *now,* when he knew he could get her on her own, could explore for himself if what he'd seen meant what he thought it did.

His sister's wedding had sparked off this burgeoning need, this awareness. He hadn't been thrown into such close proximity to Kate for years. But all through the ceremony and subsequent reception she'd held him back with that cool, frosty distance of hers. It was like being subjected to a chilly wind whistling over a deserted moor. He'd always been aware of it— yet that day, for the first time in years, it had rankled. His interest had been piqued. *Why* was she always so cool, distant?

Admittedly they had a history that up until now he'd been quite happy not to unearth. He knew on some level that that night ten years ago had marked a turning point for him, and perhaps it was one of the reasons he'd found it so easy to relegate Kate to a place he had no desire to re-explore. Her studied indifference over the years had served to keep a lid on those disturbing memories.

And yet he knew he couldn't deny the fact that he'd always been aware of her—aware of how she'd blossomed from a slightly gauche teenager into a stunningly assured and beautiful woman.

He'd thought he had that awareness and desire under control, but one night some years ago a girl had bumped into him in the street: blonde, caked in make-up, and wearing an outfit that was only a hair's breadth away from a stripper's. The feel of her body slamming into him, her huge blue eyes looking straight up into his, had scrambled his brain and fired his libido so badly that he'd sent his date home that night with some pathetic excuse and hadn't been able to look at another woman for weeks—turned on by a girl in a tarty French maid's outfit because she'd borne some resemblance to—

Tiarnan halted his wayward thoughts right there. He chafed at the resurgence of something so minor he'd thought long for- gotten—and at the implication that Kate had occupied a bigger place in his mind than he'd admitted to himself. He reassured himself that he'd had his own concerns keeping him more than occupied—and lovers who'd been only too warm and willing, making it easy to shut out the frosty indifference of one woman. Seeing Kate just once or twice a year had hardly been condu- cive to stoking the embers of a latent desire.

But just a few weeks ago…at the baptism…she'd turned and looked at him and that cool façade had dropped for the first time. She'd looked at him with such naked blatant need in those fathomless blue depths that he'd felt as if a truck had just slammed into him. For the first time Tiarnan had seen the heat of her passion under that all too cool surface. It was a heat he hadn't seen since that night, when it had combusted all around them. It could have ended so differently if he hadn't found a thread of control to cling onto.

In one instant, with one look, Tiarnan had been flung back

in time, and all attempts to keep her off limits had been made redundant. It was almost as if he'd been put to sleep after that night, and now, with a roaring, urgent sucking-in of oxygen, he was brought back to painful, aching life.

She'd clammed up again after a few moments, but it had been enough of a crack in her armour...

Blood heated and flowed thick through his veins as he took her in now. She was dressed in a dark pink silk cocktail dress, strapless, showing off the delicate line of her shoulders and collarbone, her graceful neck. Her long, luxuriant blonde hair—her trademark—hung in loose waves over her shoulders, a simple side parting framing her face. And even though he was right at the back of the room those huge blue eyes stood out. Her soft rose-pink lips were full, the firm line of her jaw and straight nose transforming banal prettiness into something much more formidable. True beauty. There was fragility in the lines of her body, and yet a sexy lushness that would have an effect on every man in that room—something Tiarnan was very aware of. Uncomfortably so.

He felt a proprietorial urge to go and sweep her off that stage and out of everyone's sight. It only firmed his resolve, strengthened his sense of right.

His eyes drifted down with leisurely and very male appreciation, taking in slender shapely legs, it was clear why she'd become one of the most sought-after models in the world. She was, quite simply, perfect. She'd become a darling of the catwalks despite their predilection for a more emaciated figure; she was the face of a well-known lingerie company among countless other campaigns. Her cool, under-the-surface sensuality meant that people sometimes described her as cold. But the problem was he knew she wasn't.

He had the personal experience to know that she was very, *very* hot.

Why had he waited so long for this?

Tiarnan clamped down on looking again at what had made him suppress his desire for so long—apart from the obvious reasons. He dismissed the rogue notion that rose unbidden and unwelcome that she'd once touched something deep within him. It must have been an illusion, borne up by the fact that they'd shared a moment in time, imbuing the experience with an enigmatic quality.

She'd displayed a self-possession at the age of eighteen that had stunned him slightly. He had to remind himself that he'd overestimated her naivety. She'd known exactly what she'd been doing then, and she was a grown woman now. Tiarnan's body tightened in anticipation. She was a woman of the world—the kind of woman he could seduce. She was no longer an innocent... A sharp pain lanced him briefly. It felt awfully like *regret,* and Tiarnan crushed it back down. He didn't do regret. He would not let her exert this sensual hold over him. He would not let her bring him back in time and reduce him to a mass of seething, frustrated desire with one look because of a *kiss!* He would seduce her and sate this lust that had been burning for too long under the surface. It was time to bring it out into the open.

All he could think about was how urgently he wanted to taste her again, touch her. She had once tried to seduce him. Now it was his turn. And this time they wouldn't stop at a kiss.

His attention came back to the proceedings. He saw Stephanides bid again. He had no intention of letting that man anywhere near Kate's lush mouth. But the Greek was stubborn and out to prove a point—especially now that he'd been informed who it was bidding against him. He and Stephanides were old adversaries. Tiarnan casually made another bid, oblivious to the gasps and looks directed at him, oblivious to the whispers that came from nearby as people speculated if it was really *him.*

People's idle speculation and chatter was of little interest to him. What was of interest was Kate Lancaster, as she stood there now, with her huge doe eyes staring straight at him but not seeing him. She would—soon enough.

Stavros Stephanides finally admitted defeat with a terse shake of his head. A sense of triumph filled Tiarnan and it was heady. He hadn't felt the sensation in a long time because triumph invariably came all too easily. With no idea as to how much he'd finally bid for a kiss with Kate, and not in the slightest bit fazed, he stepped out of the shadows and strode forward to collect his prize. Not just the kiss he was now due, but so much more. And he *would* collect—until he was sated and Kate Lancaster no longer exerted this mysterious pull over his every sense.

Kate simply didn't believe her eyes at first. *It couldn't be.* It just could not be Tiarnan Quinn striding powerfully through the seated awed crowd towards her, looking as dark and gorgeous as she'd ever seen him in a tuxedo. Her face flamed guiltily; he'd been inhabiting her dreams for weeks—and a lot longer—jeered a taunting voice, which she ignored. Only the previous night she'd woken shaken and very hot after a dream so erotic that she was sure it must be her rampant imagination conjuring him up now.

Fervently hoping that it *was* just her imagination, she took him in: the formidable build—broad shoulders, narrow hips and long legs—the loose-limbed athletic grace that hinted at his love for sports, his abhorrence of the gym. His hair was inky black, cut short, and with a slight silvering at the temples that gave him an air of sober maturity and distinction. As if he even needed it. Kate knew his darkly olive skin came from his Spanish mother. She felt weak inside, and hot.

His face was uncompromising and hard. A strong jaw and proud profile saved it from being too prettily handsome. He was intensely male—more intensely male than any man she'd ever met. Years and maturity had added to his strength, filled out his form, and it was all hard-packed muscle. But his most arresting feature was his eyes—the strongest physical hint of Celtic lineage courtesy of his Irish father. Icy blue and utterly direct. Every time he looked at her she felt as though he saw all the way through her, saw through the paltry defences she put up against him. She tried so hard to project a professional front around him, maintain her distance, knowing that if he ever came near her he'd see in an instant how tenuous her control was.

And he had. The memory sickened her. Just a month ago, at Molly's christening, he'd caught her in that unguarded moment when her naked desire for him had been painfully evident. It had been just a look, but it had been enough. He'd seen it, and ever since then she'd been having those dreams. Because she thought she'd seen a mirror of reaction in his eyes. And yet she had to be wrong. She wasn't his type—she might have been for a brief moment, a long time ago, but it had been an aberration.

A dart of familiar pain gripped her momentarily. She knew she wasn't his type because she'd seen one of his incredibly soignée girlfriends at close quarters, the memory of which made her burn with embarrassment even now. She'd been out with a group of girlfriends, visiting her in New York from Dublin, celebrating a hen night. Kate, very reluctantly, had been dressed in a French maid's outfit, complete with obligatory fishnet tights and sparkly feather duster, when she'd walked slap-bang into Tiarnan as he'd been emerging from an exclusive Madison Avenue restaurant, an arm protectively around a petite dark-haired beauty.

Kate had felt about sixteen and fled, praying that he hadn't recognised her. And then, to add insult to injury, one of her friends had chosen that moment to relieve the contents of her stomach in a gutter nearby... She'd never forget the look on Tiarnan's face, or his date's, just before they'd disappeared into the darkened interior of a waiting chauffeur-driven car.

Bitter frustration at her weak and pathetic response to him burned her inside. Would his hold over her never diminish? And now she was imagining him *here,* walking towards her, up the steps. Coming closer. Desperation made her feel panicky. When would the world right itself and the real person be revealed? Someone else. Someone who wasn't Tiarnan Quinn.

She was barely aware of the Hollywood actor speaking in awed tones beside her, but when he said the name *Tiarnan Quinn* everything seemed to zoom into focus and Kate's heart stopped altogether. Reaction set in. It *was* him—and he was now on the stage, coming closer and closer, his eyes narrowed and intent on her.

Kate's instinct where this man was concerned was always to run, as far and as fast as possible. And yet here and now she couldn't. She was caught off guard, like a deer in the headlights. And alongside the very perverse wish that she could be facing anyone else—even sleazy Stephanides—was the familiar yearning, burning feeling she got whenever this man came near.

'Kate.' His voice was deep, achingly familiar, and it impacted on her somewhere vulnerable inside, where she felt her pulse jump and her heart start again. 'Fancy meeting you here.'

Somehow she found her voice—a voice. 'Tiarnan...that was you?'

He nodded, his eyes never leaving hers. Kate had the strongest sensation that she'd been running from this man for a long time and now it was over. But in actual fact he'd caught her a long time ago. A wicked coil of something hot snaked through her belly even as she clamped down desperately on every emotion and any outward sign of his effect on her.

With a smooth move she didn't see coming, Tiarnan came close and put his hands around her waist, thumbs disturbingly close to the undersides of her breasts. His touch was so shocking after years of avoiding any contact beyond the most perfunctory that she automatically put her hands out to steady herself, and found herself clasping his upper arms. Powerful muscles were evident underneath the expensive cloth of his suit. Her belly melted and she looked up helplessly, still stunned to be facing him like this. Shock was rendering her usual defences around him useless.

He was so tall; he'd always been one of the few men that she had to look up to, even in the highest of heels. He towered over her now, making her feel small, delicate. She was aware of every slow second passing, aware of their breaths, but she knew rationally that things were happening in real time, and that no one was aware of the undercurrents flowing between them. At least she hoped they weren't.

'I believe you owe me a kiss?'

This was said lightly, but Tiarnan's grip on her waist was warm and firm, warning her not to try and run or shirk her duty. She nodded, feeling utterly bewildered; what else could she do in front of the wealthiest, most powerful people in San Francisco? How much had he paid in the end? She'd forgotten already. But it had been a shockingly high amount. Half a million dollars? She had the very strong feeling that he was claiming far more than a kiss, and that coil of heat burned fiercer within her.

He pulled her closer, until their bodies were almost touching, and all Kate could feel was that heat—within her and around her. It climbed up her chest and into her face as Tiarnan's head lowered. Overwhelmed at being ambushed like this, and feeling very bewildered, Kate fluttered her eyes closed as the man she'd failed so abysmally to erase from her memory banks pressed his firm, sensual mouth against hers. It had been ten years since they'd kissed like this, and suddenly Kate was eighteen again, pressing her lips ardently against his...

Kate put a shaky finger to her mouth, which still felt sensitive. As kisses went it had been chaste enough, fleeting enough, but the effect had been pure devastation. She'd been hurtled back in time and Pandora's Box was now wide open. A flare of guilt assailed her; she'd fled the thronged ballroom as soon as she'd had the chance.

They'd been grabbed for photos with the press pack behind the stage straight after Tiarnan had claimed his kiss. Dizzy with the after-effects, she'd stood there smiling inanely. His hand had been warm on her elbow, his presence overwhelming. It was still a complete mystery to her as to why he was here at all, but she hadn't even had the wherewithal to stick around and make small talk. She'd run. Exactly like that night in New York on the street.

Bitter recrimination burned her. She was falling apart every time she saw him now, and if she'd not already made an ass of herself in France, mooning at him like a lovesick groupie, then tonight would certainly have him wondering what on earth was wrong with her. How was it possible that instead of growing immune to him she was growing ever more aware of him? Where was the law of physics in that?

She'd fled, not really thinking about where she was going, and now she realised that she was in the hotel bar, with its floor-to-ceiling windows showcasing a glittering view of downtown San Francisco in all its night-time vibrancy. The sound of a siren wailing somewhere nearby failed to root her in reality. The bar was blissfully dark and quiet. A pianist played soothing jazz in the corner. Kate took a seat at a table by the window. After a few minutes someone approached her. She looked up, thinking it would be the waiter, but it was a stranger—a man. He was wearing a suit and looked a little the worse for wear.

'Excuse me, but me and my buddies—' he gestured behind him to two other men in crumpled suits at the bar, who waved cheerfully '—we're all agreed that you're the prettiest woman we've ever seen. Can we buy you a drink?'

Kate smiled tightly, her nerve ends jangling. 'Thanks, really…but if you don't mind I'm happy to get my own drink.'

He swayed unsteadily, with a look of affront on his face, before lurching back to his friends. Then she saw one of the other men make a move towards her, as if taking up the baton. She cursed her impulse to come here, and turned her face resolutely to the window, hoping that would deter him.

She heard a movement, a deep voice, and then a looming dark shape materialised in the glass. She looked up and saw the face of her dreams reflected above her own. Disembodied. Throat dry, she looked round and up. Tiarnan stood there, looking straight at her, eyes like blue shards of ice against his dark skin. Her heart leapt; her palms dampened.

A waitress appeared next to him, and when she asked if they'd like a drink Tiarnan just looked at Kate and said, 'Two Irish whiskeys?'

Kate nodded helplessly, and watched as Tiarnan took the seat opposite her, undoing his bow tie as he did so and opening the top button on his shirt with easy insouciance. His voice, that distinctive accent with its unmistakable Irish roots, affected her somewhere deep inside. It was a connection they shared—both being half Irish and brought up in Ireland.

He jerked his head back towards the men sitting at the bar. 'You could have sent me packing too. They must be devastated.'

A dart of irritation and anger sparked through Kate at Tiarnan, for being here and upsetting her equilibrium. Her voice came out tight. 'I know you. I don't know them.'

His brow quirked. A hint of a smile played around his mouth. Kate felt very exposed in her strapless dress. Her breasts felt full against the bodice. She strove for calm, to be polite, urbane. This was her best friend's brother, that was all. They'd bumped into each other. That was all. On the surface of things. She wouldn't think about what was happening under the surface, the minefield of history that lay buried there. She smiled, but it felt brittle.

'What brings you to San Francisco, Tiarnan?'

Tiarnan's eyes narrowed. He could see very well that Kate was retreating into that cool shell he knew so well. The shell that for years had deflected his attention, made him believe she didn't desire him. But he knew better now, and he saw the pulse under the pale skin of her neck beat hectically even as she projected a front so glacial he could swear the temperature had dropped a few degrees.

He fought the urge to say, *You,* and instead drawled, 'Business. Sorcha mentioned you were here for the annual Buchanen Cancer benefit.' He shrugged easily deciding not to divulge the fact that he'd specifically booked into the same hotel as her. 'I'm staying here too, so I thought I'd come look for you. It would appear that I found you just in time.'

A vision of being kissed and groped by Stavros Stephanides came back into Kate's head. She lowered her head slightly. Some hair slipped forward over her shoulder. She longed for something to cover herself up, and berated herself for not going straight to her room. What had compelled her to come here? She forced herself to look up. She couldn't go anywhere now.

'Yes. I never thanked you for that.' And then curiosity got the better of her. 'How much did you pay in the end?'

'You don't remember?

Kate burned as she shook her head, knowing very well why she didn't remember.

He seemed to savour his words. 'Seven hundred and fifty thousand dollars. And worth every cent.'

It would be. Tiarnan watched her reaction, the shock on her beautiful face, those amazing blue eyes framed with the longest black lashes. Saw the way the candlelight flickered over her satin smooth skin, the slope of her shoulders, the swell of her breasts above the dress. His body hardened and Tiarnan shifted, uncomfortably aware that he wasn't used to women having such an immediate effect on him. He enjoyed always being in control, and yet he could already feel that control becoming a little shaky, elusive… Sitting here with Kate now, the thrill of anticipation was headier than anything he'd felt in a long time.

He'd paid over half a million dollars, just like that. The amount staggered Kate, and yet she knew to Tiarnan it was like small change. That was a fraction of what he gave to charity every year.

'At least it's for a good cause,' she said a little shakily.

The waitress arrived then, with two glasses. She placed napkins down, and then the drinks, and left.

Tiarnan reached out a strong, long-fingered hand and raised his glass towards her, an enigmatic gleam in his eyes. 'A very good cause.'

Kate raised her glass too and clinked it off his. She had the very disturbing impression that they weren't talking about the same thing. Just then his fingers touched hers, and a memory flashed into her head: her arms wrapped tight around his neck, tongues touching and tasting. Tiarnan's hands moving to her buttocks, pulling her in tight so she could feel the thrillingly hard ridge of his arousal. She could almost hear their heartbeats, slow and heavy, then picking up pace, drowning out their breathing—

Kate jerked her hand back so quickly that some of her drink slopped out of the glass. Her skin felt stretched tight, hot. She couldn't believe this was happening. It was like her worst nightmare and her most fervent dream.

She took a quick sip, all the while watching Tiarnan as he watched her, hoping that he couldn't read the turmoil in her head, in her chest. The whiskey trickled like liquid velvet down her throat. She wasn't used to this, that was all. Tiarnan didn't seek her out. She only ever saw him with Sorcha, or when lots of people were around. When Sorcha had lived with her in New York and Tiarnan had called round or invited them out to dinner Kate had always made an excuse, always made sure she wasn't there as much as possible.

But facing him now…that kiss earlier… She was helpless to escape the images threatening to burst through the walls she'd placed around them. Tiarnan leant back, stretching out his long legs, cradling his glass as if this were completely normal, as if they met like this all the time. The latent strength in his body was like a tangible thing.

Kate had to close her eyes for a second as she battled against a vision of him pulling back from kissing her, breathing harshly—

'So, Kate, how have you been?'

Her eyes snapped open. What was *wrong* with her? Normally she managed to keep all this under control, but it was almost as if some silent communication was going on that she knew nothing about—something subversive that she was not in control of, messing with her head. She'd never been so tense. But she told herself she could do this—do the small-talk thing. And after this drink she'd make her excuses and get up and walk away—not see Tiarnan for another few months, or even a year if she was lucky.

So she nodded her head and smiled her most professional smile, injecting breeziness into her voice. 'Fine. Great! Wasn't Molly's christening just gorgeous? I can't believe how big she is already. Sorcha and Romain are so happy. Have you seen them since? I've been *crazy* busy. I had to go to South America straight after the baptism. I got back a few days ago and I flew in tonight for the benefit—'

She took a deep, audibly shaky breath, intending to keep going with her monologue, thinking *Just talk fast and get out of here even faster,* when Tiarnan leant forward and said with quiet emphasis, 'Kate—stop.'

CHAPTER TWO

KATE'S mouth opened and closed. With just those two words she knew that he was seeing right through her—*again*. Silly tears pricked the backs of her eyes. He was playing with her, mocking her for her weakness, as if he'd known all along. So she asked the question, even though she knew it would give her away completely,

'Tiarnan, what are you *really* doing here?'

His face was shuttered, eyes unreadable. The dim lights cast him half in shadow, making him look dark and dangerous. Like a Spanish pirate. His shoulders looked huge. Kate's insides ached as only the way a body recognising its mate ached. Its other half.

Her soft mouth compressed. She'd tried to tell herself that what had happened between them hadn't been unique, hadn't been as earth-shattering as she remembered, but…it had. Since that night, no one had ever kissed her the way he had—with such devastating skill that she'd never been able to get over him. He'd imprinted himself so deeply into her cells. Just one kiss, a mere moment, that was all it had been, but it had been enough.

She repeated the question now, a throb of desperation mixed with anger in her voice, even leaned forward, put her glass down. She wanted to shout at him to just leave her alone, let her get on with her life so she could realise her dream: find someone to love. Have a family. *Finally get over him.*

'What are you doing here, Tiarnan? We both know—'

'We both know why I'm here.' His voice was harsh. The piano player was between numbers, and the words hung almost accusingly in the soft silence. Time seemed to hang suspended, and then the piano player started again and so did Kate's heart, and she desperately tried to claw back some self control and pretend that he *wasn't* referring to that night.

'I don't know what you're talking about.'

Tiarnan took a swift drink and leaned forward to put his empty glass down on the table. The sound made Kate flinch inside.

'You know perfectly well what I'm talking about. That explicit look you gave me in France, and what *didn't* happen that night.'

Oh, God. Kate felt the colour drain from her face. She was officially in her worst nightmare. She *knew* he'd seen her weakness in France—but she just hadn't been able to hide it. And if Tiarnan Quinn was known for anything, it was for sensing weakness and exploiting it ruthlessly.

She forced herself to meet his gaze, even though it was hard, and her voice came out low and husky. 'That night was a long time ago—and you're right. Nothing happened—' She stopped ineffectually. What could she say? *If you're thinking if I still want you, even after a humiliating rejection, then you're right.* Bitterness rose within her.

He was still sitting forward—predatory, dangerous. He said softly, in that deep voice, 'I'd call that kiss something happening, and that look told me that you've been just as aware of this build-up of sexual tension as I have.'

Kate shook her head fiercely, as if that could negate this whole experience. Shame coursed through her again at her youthful naivety, and yet her body tingled even now, when humiliation hung over her like the Sword of Damocles.

Why was he bringing this up *now?* Was he bored? Did he think he'd seen an invitation in her eyes that day at the christening? She burned inside at the thought and rushed to try and fill the silence, the gap, to regain some dignity.

'Tiarnan, like I said, it was a long time ago. I barely remember it, and I've no intention of ever talking about it or repeating the experience. I was very young.'

And a virgin. That unwanted spiking of regret shocked Tiarnan again, and suddenly the thought of other men looking at her, touching her, made him feel almost violent...

He said nothing for a long moment. He couldn't actually speak as he looked into clear blue eyes not dissimilar to his own. They were like drops of ice but they couldn't cool him down. Tiarnan fought the urge to reach across the table and pull her up, crush her mouth under his, taste her again. Instead he finally said, 'You're a liar, and that's a pity.'

Kate felt winded, breathless. The way he was looking at her was so *hot*—but she didn't think for a second that it meant anything. She didn't know why he was bringing this up now. She just wanted to stay in one piece until she could get away.

'I'm not a liar,' she asserted, and then frowned when she registered what he'd said. 'And what do you mean, it's a pity?'

Tiarnan sat back again, and perversely that made Kate more nervous than when he'd been closer.

'You're a liar because I believe you *do* remember every second of that kiss, as well as I do, and it's a pity you don't intend repeating it because I'd very much like to.'

Kate sat straight and tall. Somewhere dimly she could hear her mother's strident voice in her head: *Kate Lancaster, sit up straight. I won't have you let me down with sloppy manners. Show your breeding. You're a young lady and you will not embarrass me in front of these people!*

Her focus returned to the room. She wasn't ten years old. She was twenty-eight. She was an internationally renowned model: successful, independent. She struggled to cling onto what was real: the pianist was playing a familiar tune, the dark, muted tones of the bar, the lights glittering and twinkling out-side. The waitress appeared again, and Kate could see Tiarnan gesture for another drink. His eyes hadn't left hers, and she thought that she might have misheard him. He might have said something entirely different. But then she remembered the way his hands had felt around her waist earlier, how close his thumbs had brushed to her breasts. The way he'd looked at her. The way he was looking at her now.

Ten years on from one moment with this man and she was a quivering wreck. Despite a full and busy life, despite relation-ships... If he had decided, for whatever reason, that he wanted her, and if she acquiesced, it would be like opening the door, flinging her arm wide with a smile on her face and inviting ca-tastrophe to move in for ever. If she was this bad after a kiss, what would she be like after succumbing to the sensual invita-tion that was in his eyes right now? Because that look said that a kiss would be the very least of the experience. And awfully, treacherously, any insecurity she'd harboured since that night about her own sexual appeal died a death in a flame of heat. But it was small comfort. He had rejected her clumsy, innocent advances and she had to remember that—no matter how he might be making her feel right now.

The fact that this moment was a direct manifestation of her most secret fantasies was making her reel. The waitress came and deposited more drinks, taking away the empty glasses. Kate shook her head, feeling her hair move across too sensi-tive skin. She knew all about Tiarnan Quinn—she'd always known all about him. One of the perks of being best friends with his sister. So Kate knew well how he compartmentalised women, how he inevitably left them behind. She'd witnessed his ruthless control first-hand. She wouldn't, *couldn't* allow that to happen again. Not even when his softly spoken words had set up a chain reaction in her body that she'd been ignoring for the past few earth-shattering seconds.

She shook her head harder, even smiled faintly, as if sharing in a joke, as if this whole evening wasn't costing her everything.

'I don't think you mean that for a second.' She took a drink from her glass, put it down again and looked at Tiarnan. 'And even if you did, like I said, I've no desire to re-enact that kiss for your amusement. If all you're looking for is a convenient woman, there are plenty available. You don't need me. I don't think I need to remind you that you made your rejection of my advances quite plain that night.'

Tiarnan chafed at her sudden assuredness—and at her reminder of his clumsy rejection. That feeling of regret spiked uncomfortably again. Her smile was almost mocking—as if she pitied him! He'd never been an object of pity, and he wasn't about to start being one now.

He smiled tightly and saw Kate's eyes widen, the pulse trip in her throat.

'I rejected you because you were inexperienced, too young, and my little sister's best friend.' His jaw clenched. '*Not* because I didn't desire you, as you may well remember. I'm looking for a lot more than a re-enactment of that kiss, and believe me, I don't expect it to be amusing. I'm not looking for a convenient lay, Kate. I'm looking for *you.*'

All of Kate's precious composure crumbled at his raw words.

'You can't possibly mean that...that you—'

'Want you?' He almost grimaced, as if in pain. 'I want you, Kate. As much as you want me.'

'I don't.' she breathed.

He arched a brow. 'No? Then what was that look about at the christening, when you all but devoured me with your hungry blue eyes? And the way you trembled earlier under my hands?'

Kate flushed brick-red. 'Stop it. I wasn't. I didn't.' This was too cruel. Her humiliation knew no bounds. The sword had fallen spectacularly.

Tiarnan grimaced again. 'Don't worry. It's mutual.' His blue eyes speared hers. 'You've never forgotten that night, Kate, have you? It's why you always freeze me out every time we meet.'

She shook her head, his intuition sending shockwaves through her whole body. 'Don't be ridiculous. It was so long ago...of course I've...' She hitched up her chin defiantly. 'I've more than kissed men since then, Tiarnan. What did you think? That I've hugged my pillow to sleep every night, dreaming of you?'

The awful thing was, she could remember the mortification that had led her to rid herself of her virginity as soon as was humanly possible after that night—and what an excruciating disappointment it had been.

His mouth had become a thin line of displeasure. 'I wouldn't imagine for a second that you haven't had lovers, Kate.'

He reached out and took her hand, gripped it so that she couldn't pull away, and Kate was caught, trapped by her own weak responses: lust, and the building of guilty exhilaration. Her heart beat frantically against her breastbone.

'But did any of them make you feel the way I did after just a kiss? Did any of them make you want them so badly that it was all you could think about? Dream about?'

Tiarnan felt momentarily shocked by his words and the emotion behind them; until recently, until he'd set on this course to seduce Kate, he'd never really allowed himself to acknowledge what her effect on him had been. Touching her now, confronting this for the first time, was bringing it all back in vivid detail. Her hand felt small, soft and yet strong. He could feel her pulse beating under the skin.

Kate saw a red mist descend. The exhilaration dissipated. His words were so close to the bone—*too* close to the bone. She pulled her hand from his grasp and curled it tight against her chest.

'How dare you? How dare you come back into my life like this, making assumptions? Judgements? Asking me about things you've no right to know?'

Tiarnan looked at her and felt more sure than ever.

'I have a right, Kate, because one kiss clearly wasn't enough. This has been building between us all these years...this *desire* to know what it might have been like.'

Anger rushed through her, gathering force, and she used it before she could dissolve again. She stood up on shaky legs and looked down as imperiously as she could. But then Tiarnan stood too, altering the dynamic, taking some of the fire out of her anger, making her remember just how tall he was, how broad and strong.

She hitched her chin. 'I think *dormant* is a more appropriate word, and dormant is how it'll stay, Tiarnan. What's brought on this revelation? The fact that you thought you saw something in France? You saw nothing except what you wanted to see. I've no intention of becoming a notch on your bedpost just to satisfy some belated curiosity on your part.'

She walked around the table, as if to leave, but Tiarnan moved too and blocked her way. Kate saw a couple of people looking at them in her peripheral vision. She stalled and looked up, tried to shut out the way looking into Tiarnan's eyes had always made her feel as if she was drowning. She gritted her teeth.

'Could you please move? You're blocking my exit.'

'Need I remind you,' he said silkily, 'that *you* were the one so determined to score that notch in the first place? We both know that if I hadn't stopped when I still could I would have taken your innocence on the rug in front of that fire...'

Those softly spoken words smashed through the last vestiges of Kate's dignity and defence. She looked up at him and beseeched with everything in her. 'Please. Get out of my way, Tiarnan.'

He shook his head. 'I'm walking you to your room.'

'I'm perfectly capable of walking myself, and have been for some time now.'

His voice had steel running through it. 'Nevertheless, I'll walk you to your room—or do you want me to make a spectacle of both of us and carry you out of here?'

One jet-black brow was arched. Kate didn't doubt him for a second. Tiarnan had never been one to give a damn about what people thought.

She felt unbelievably prim as she bit out, 'That won't be necessary. You can escort me to my room if you insist.'

He finally moved aside to let her pass, and Kate stalked towards the entrance of the bar feeling stiff all over, her shoulders so straight and tense that she felt as if she'd crack if someone even touched her. She pressed the button for the lift and looked resolutely up at the display above the door as she waited. Tiarnan stood beside her, a huge, impossibly immovable force. Heat and electricity crackled between them. There was such tension in the air that Kate wanted to scream.

No one reduced her to this. *No one.* She was dignified, calm, collected. She knew she had a reputation for being cool and it hurt her—she was the least cold of people. She could turn it on when it suited her, but it wasn't really her. Cold histrionics and dramatics had been the territory of her mother. Kate had learnt at an early age to be a pretty, placid foil for her mother's effervescent beauty.

The lift arrived and the bell pinged, making Kate jump and then curse silently. She hadn't thought about her mother like that for a long time; Tiarnan's disturbing presence and even more disturbing assertions were effortlessly hurtling her back in time.

He stepped into the lift with her, and the space contracted around them when the doors closed. Kate pressed the button for her floor and looked at Tiarnan irritably when he didn't make a move to do the same. 'Which floor?'

Tiarnan looked at her glaring up at him. She was so beautiful. All fire and brimstone underneath that icy façade. Her eyes were flashing, her cheeks were pink and her breasts rose and fell enticingly under the bodice of her dress. She was rattled, seriously rattled, and he had to admit he was surprised at what was so close to the surface.

In truth he'd imagined this happening much more easily. He'd imagined a sophisticated woman embarking on a well-worn groove, both of them knowing and acting out their parts. But right now he was rattled too. She was resisting him. He couldn't think. All he wanted was to stop the lift, drag her into his arms and plunder her soft mouth. It had been too long since he'd tasted that inner sweetness, and the brief all too chaste kiss earlier had only proved to make his desire even more pronounced. But he knew he couldn't. He had to tread carefully or he might lose Kate for ever—and he didn't like the panicky feeling that generated. He didn't *do* panic.

Kate turned and folded her arms crossly, inadvertently giving Tiarnan an even more enticing view of her cleavage. She was sending out desperate silent vibes: *Get away from me! Leave me alone!* And as the lift climbed the floors with excruciating slowness that was exactly what he did. He actually moved further away. Back towards the wall. And when Kate sent him a suspicious glance she saw that he was leaning back, hands in his pockets, looking at the ceiling. He was even whistling softly.

The lift finally came to a smooth halt and Kate all but ran out through the doors, taking her door key from her purse as she did so. She expected him to be right behind her. She'd seen a new side to him tonight: implacable, ruthless. Determined. It intimidated her. *It excited her.* She got to her door and slid the key into the slot, her hands barely steady after that revelation.

But if he thought for a second that she was going to meekly turn around now and invite him in— Kate turned and pasted on a bright smile, words trembling on her lips…only to find the corridor empty. For a split second she had the bizarre and terrifying notion that she'd imagined the whole thing. Dreamt it all up.

But then she saw him. Leaning against the open lift door nonchalantly, one foot stopping it from closing, his huge shoulders blocking the light inside. That was why she hadn't seen him straight away. He inclined his head,

'Goodnight, Kate, it was good to see you again. Sweet dreams.'

And with that he stepped back in and the doors closed with a swish. Kate's mouth dropped open. All she could see in her mind's eye was that nonchalance and the bright dangerous glitter of blue eyes under dark brows. All her pent-up fury dissolved and she literally sagged like a spent balloon. She stepped inside her door and closed it, stood with her back against it in the dark for a long moment. Her heart beat fast, her skin tingled and her lips still felt sensitive. And yet more than all this was the ache of desire. She felt raw, as if a wound had been reopened.

Damn Tiarnan Quinn. He was playing her—playing with her. She didn't believe for a second that he was going to meekly walk away. No more than she would have meekly let him into her room. He was undoubtedly the most Alpha male she'd ever known. He always had been. He'd been born Alpha. And she'd set him a challenge with her refusal to acknowledge what had happened between them. There was no sense of excitement in knowing this, no sense of anticipation. She'd been too badly hurt in the past. She'd spent too long disguising her feelings, pretending to herself that she didn't want him. Hiding it from others, even from Sorcha.

She couldn't help but feel—knowing his reputation, which was legendary albeit discreet—that she was posing a challenge to him in large part because he'd let her get away. Was this the banal satisfaction of some long-forgotten curiosity? Kate knew well that there would be a very small number on Tiarnan Quinn's list of women who had resisted his charms, for whatever reason. She had the uncanny prescience that hers might be the only name. And yet that night it had been *he* who had stopped proceedings, not her. He was absolutely right; if she'd had any say that night ten years ago they would have made love on that rug in front of the fire.

For whatever reason, he'd obviously decided that he wanted to carry on from where they'd left off. And Kate knew with every bone in her body that if she didn't resist him she would be the biggest fool on this earth. The one shred of dignity she'd clung onto all these years was the very fact that they hadn't slept together.

Tiarnan stood at the window of the sitting room in his luxurious suite. The best in the hotel. He felt hot and frustrated, hands deep in the pockets of his trousers as he looked out at the view, not seeing a bit of it.

All he could see was his own reflection in the window and the slightly tortured look on his face—tortured because Kate Lancaster was lying in bed some floors below him in the very same hotel, and right now Tiarnan would have gladly given over half his fortune to be in that bed with her. She'd emerged from the mists of memory to assume a place that no other woman had ever assumed.

He could smell Kate's light floral scent even now. And yet she'd walked away, resisted him. Tiarnan couldn't remember a time when any woman he'd wanted had resisted him. From the moment the divorced wife of one of his father's friends had seduced him as a teenager he'd seen the manipulative side to women and had been initiated into their ways.

His mother had dealt him his first lesson. Cold and martyred. He'd seen how she'd made life hell for his father. Not happy to have been brought to inclement Ireland from her native Spain, she'd subjected his father and him to the frost of her discontent, eventually driving his father into the arms of another woman who'd been only too happy to accommodate him. Tiarnan could remember his father's secretary, how she would cajole and plead with him to marry *her.* He'd witnessed those scenes as he'd played outside his father's office, listening to the crying and hysterics. And then she'd taken the drastic step of becoming pregnant in a bid to secure her own happiness, and Tiarnan had been forced to collude in a devastating lie.

He forced his mind away from dark memories. He'd witnessed too much as a child. He knew well enough that his father had been no innocent party, but the machinations of the first female role models in his life had inured him to their ways and moods as he'd grown up. He'd vowed long ago not to be at the mercy of any woman, and yet despite everything, all his lessons learnt, he'd been caught too. Rage still simmered down low in acknowledgement of that.

A ripple of cynicism went through him. Even in Kate's innocence ten years ago she'd been manipulative too, just like the rest. Her innocence had been hidden beneath a veneer of sophistication that had fooled him completely until the moment he'd felt that hesitation. A telling gaucheness, an untutored response. It had cut through the haze of lust that had clouded his judgment that night.

Tiarnan could remember the spiking of betrayal and desperation he'd felt. He'd believed her to be experienced. For a second he'd been seduced into believing them to be on equal ground, both knowing what was happening.

Certainly there'd been no indication when she'd found him alone in the library. He'd offered her a drink and she'd taken it… Her hair had gleamed like spun gold in the firelight. A storm had howled outside. There had been a Christmas party going on in the house. Tiarnan had been making a rare home visit…

She had been wearing a dark red silk dress. Ruched and short, it had clung to her breasts and the curve of her hips. Her long legs had been bare, she'd worn high heels. She had taken the glass of whiskey and smiled at him, and for the first time Tiarnan had allowed himself to really notice her. In truth he'd noticed her as soon as he'd arrived that evening, and he hadn't been able to take his eyes off her. Some defence of his must have been down.

He'd noticed her before—of course he had—he'd have to have been dead not to. But strictly as his sister's friend. They'd both been tall and gangly, giggling blushing girls, but that night for the first time Tiarnan had seen that Kate had become a woman.

It was a quality that his own almost eighteen-year-old sister still hadn't quite achieved. But he'd had to concede that Kate had always possessed a quiet air of mature dignity, of inherent sophistication. A quiet foil to Sorcha's rowdiness and effervescence. Sorcha, his sister, had just come through a traumatic time after the relatively recent death of their father, and Tiarnan had taken the opportunity to thank Kate for being there for her.

Kate had blushed and looked down into her glass before looking back up, something fierce in her eyes. 'I love Sorcha. She's the closest thing I have to a sister and I'd do anything for her.'

Tiarnan could remember smiling at her, seeing her eyes widen in response, and then the flare of his arousal had hit so strong and immediate that it had nearly knocked him sideways. The air around them had changed in an instant, crackling with sexual tension. Even though Tiarnan had tried to deny it, to regain some sanity.

Standing there with her skin glowing in the firelight, her lush body firing his senses… He could remember how choked his voice had felt with the need to push her away when all he'd wanted to do was kiss her into oblivion.

'You know I've always considered *you* like a sister too, Kate.'

For an infinitesimal moment Kate had just looked at him, and then she'd carefully put down the drink and come closer to him, her blue eyes glittering, pupils huge. And she'd said huskily, 'I don't see you as a brother, Tiarnan. And I don't want you to see me as a sister.'

His arousal had sky-rocketed. On some level Tiarnan hadn't been able to believe he was being so wound up by an *eighteen-year-old girl*. But in fairness she wasn't like other eighteen-year-olds. She'd already been a model for a couple of years, was already living independently in London. And he couldn't believe she was standing there and seducing him. Or how out of his depth he felt in that moment. At the age of twenty-eight he was no novice around women, but he'd felt like one then.

She'd stepped right up to him and placed her hands around his face. Then, stretching up, she'd pressed her mouth to his. He'd put his hands on her waist, to try and set her back—but he'd felt her curves, and then she'd leaned closer into him, her soft breasts pressed against his chest…and he'd been lost. From that moment Tiarnan had been overtaken for the first time in his life by pure, unadulterated lust. It had felt like the most necessary thing in the world to pull her even closer, to deepen the kiss, taste her with his tongue.

Things had become heated and urgent in seconds, and only that telling movement she'd made, which had brought him back to sanity, had stopped the night ending a lot differently.

Tiarnan's focus came back from the heat of that memory. The vividness of it shocked him. He knew if he was asked he wouldn't be able to recall his last sexual liaison with such clarity. He stepped away from the window with a jerky movement and did the only thing he could do to ensure he'd have a modicum of sleep that night. He took a cold shower and vowed to himself as he did so that very soon he'd have Kate Lancaster in his bed—once that had happened these provocative memories would return to where they belonged: in the past.

Madrid, one week later

'Signorina Lancaster, you have a call.'

The phone felt slippery in Kate's hand. She knew who it was, and her body was already responding as if he was right there in the room with her.

'Gracias.'

She heard a click on the line and then a voice, deep, authoritative. 'Kate.'

His voice reached right down inside her and caused a quiver. She pressed her legs together and gripped the phone even tighter.

'Tiarnan. What a surprise.'

'Hardly,' he responded drily. 'I live about ten minutes from your hotel, and Sorcha told me you'd got the messages I've left. Apparently you've been too busy to get back to me.'

'I did speak to her earlier—and, yes, I've been extremely busy.'

'But now you're finished working?'

'Yes.' Relief rushed through her. Escape was in sight. She was still getting over the shock of having been sent on this last-minute assignment to Madrid—right into Tiarnan's territory, and so soon after their last meeting. Which she had no intention of repeating.

'I'm going home tomorrow—'

'Evening,' Tiarnan finished smoothly for her. 'So you have plenty of time to let us take you for lunch tomorrow.'

'I'm afraid I—' Kate stopped. He'd said *us*.

'Rosie is here. She'd like to see you.'

The words of a lame excuse died in Kate's throat. As much as she hated him for doing this to her, she knew that he would never in a million years use Rosie in any kind of manipulative way. He would know that she'd spent time with Rosie, but probably had very little idea just how much. Kate liked Rosie. She'd used to help Sorcha look after her whenever Tiarnan was in New York on business—which had been frequently enough, as he had offices there. He had sometimes left Rosie with Sorcha for a night or two a couple of times a year when she'd been younger. It had always turned into a joint effort, as Sorcha had been living with Kate in New York until just before she'd met her husband.

Sorcha, up until her pregnancy and the birth of her own daughter, hadn't possessed a maternal bone in her body, so Kate had always been the one to make sure Rosie was wrapped up warm, had eaten well and was tucked in at night. Sorcha used to joke that Kate had been born with a double helping of maternal instinct to make up for the lack of her mother's. The three of them would go to Central Park on adventures, or to the movies and for ice cream afterwards. Kate had always felt a kinship with the small, serious dark-haired child, whose mother had all but abandoned her after her divorce from Tiarnan.

'I'd like to see Rosie too. It's been a while.' Kate's voice felt husky, and already in her head she was rationalising giving in. She *was* leaving tomorrow evening, and with Rosie at lunch too Tiarnan was hardly going to ravish her, was he? And then once she got back to New York she'd be safe again…it would be fine.

'Good. We'll pick you up at midday from the lobby. See you then, Kate.'

And with those softly spoken last words, almost like a caress, the phone line went dead and Kate had the horrible feeling that everything was *not* going to be fine.

CHAPTER THREE

THE following day at midday Kate sat in the lobby of the impossibly chic hotel where she'd been staying. She'd already said goodbye to the crew who'd been with her for the shoot. They were all leaving on an earlier flight, heading to London and their next assignment. Her nerves were coiled tight, making her belly constrict. The thought of the lunch ahead was daunting, to say the least.

And then, as if pulled by an invisible thread, Kate's head came up and she saw Tiarnan silhouetted in the doorway. A huge, imposing figure. Not even giving her time to collect herself, prepare herself. Kate's nerves intensified to a crescendo as she stood up jerkily. Tiarnan strode authoritatively towards her—a man clearly on his own turf. Confident, powerful.

He was dressed in black trousers and a white shirt, open at the neck, his dark skin visible and the strong bronzed column of his throat. Kate hadn't been sure what to wear, and her wardrobe was limited, so she'd gone for a plain black shirt dress and accessorised it with a bright red scarf around her throat. She'd pulled her hair back in a ponytail, trying to project an image that said *friend* and not *lover.* Except right now she felt as if her scarf was strangling her as Tiarnan came to a halt right in front of her. *Too close.* Especially when he took her hands and leant forward to kiss her on both cheeks.

His scent wound through her, and she felt that quiver between her legs again. He had his own very uniquely male scent. She'd always been aware of it. He was one of the few men she knew who didn't douse himself in cologne. Kate had developed an acute sensitivity to smell after years of having to promote various perfumes, almost to the point that strong scents made her feel ill. But Tiarnan's scent was simply soap and water and *him*. Headier than any manufactured scent.

He let her hands go and they tingled. He looked around her. 'Where are your things?'

Kate fought to sound calm, aloof. 'The concierge has my bag. I've arranged for a car to pick me up from here to go to the airport later.'

Tiarnan shook his head and took her by the elbow to lead her over to the desk. 'That won't be necessary.'

In shock, Kate heard him instruct the concierge to cancel the cab and get her bag. The man jumped straight away, clearly recognising Tiarnan. She rounded on him, incensed that he was already dictating. 'What do you think you're doing?'

He looked down at her, leaning nonchalantly against the concierge desk. 'I have to go to the airport later too. You might as well come with me. It'll give us more time together.'

Kate realised something then. Suspicion sparked from her eyes and she crossed her arms. 'Where's Rosie?'

Tiarnan straightened as Kate's small case was delivered by the concierge, who all but bowed to Tiarnan.

He took Kate's arm again, giving her no choice but to trot after him unless she wanted to create a scene. She felt slightly bewildered. She wasn't used to seeing this side of Tiarnan. They emerged, and Kate saw a Range Rover and realised that he still hadn't answered her question. He opened the passenger door and turned to her, the intense blue of his eyes rendering her speechless.

'Rosie's at home. I thought we'd have lunch there.'

She chafed at his easy dominance, at the feeling of being backed into a corner. Tiarnan still had a hand on her elbow and he helped her into the passenger seat. Then, after putting her case in the back, he came around and got into the front, pulling away from the hotel with smooth ease.

The journey to Tiarnan's home didn't take long. It was in the Salamanca area of Madrid, one of the oldest *barrios* and home to some of the most exclusive houses, shops and hotels. It was just off Calle de Serrano, near a charming park, where he turned into a set of huge wrought-iron gates which opened slowly.

Kate looked around her, seriously impressed. Madrid was one of her favourite cities—it always had been. She loved its vibrancy, its history, the café culture, and could spend days wandering around, taking in the museums and galleries. Even now, though it was well into autumn, people were strolling in the lingering warm sunshine. Tiarnan waited to let a woman pass with a baby in a pushchair, and Kate had a sudden vision of what it might be like to live here, have this life. *Be that woman with the pushchair.*

She glanced at Tiarnan's profile as he drove forward when the gates were fully open. He looked distant, and not a little harsh. A shiver went through her even as she felt hot inside. He'd never be part of a dream like that. He'd made it clear a long time ago that as far as he was concerned he'd done the family thing. Sorcha had often told Kate how strongly Tiarnan felt about never marrying again. How Rosie had fulfilled any need he might have had for children.

'Here we are.'

Kate's turbulent thoughts came to an abrupt halt when she realised that they'd stopped outside a huge baroque townhouse. The colour of warm sandstone, it had a crumbling grandeur, with wooden shutters held back from gleaming windows. Bright flowers burst from ornate wrought-iron window box railings and from pots set around the steps and door. Trees surrounded the house, so that it seemed to nestle into the foliage. It was beautiful.

Tiarnan came around to join her. He carried her case in one hand. Kate asked suspiciously, 'Why are you taking it out of the car?'

Tiarnan's blue gaze mocked her for her suspicion. 'Because my driver Juan will be taking us to the airport.'

'But how do you know what time I have to be there?' Kate was struggling not to give in to Tiarnan's effortless domination.

His mouth quirked and her belly flipped.

'Because I know everything, Kate. Stop worrying. I'm not going to jump on you like some callow youth. You're quite safe.'

Just then the massive front door opened, and Kate saw a small dark-haired figure appear. Genuine emotion rushed through her. Tiarnan was forgotten for a moment.

'Rosie!'

Kate started forward instinctively, but then faltered. Rosie wasn't running to greet her as Kate remembered she'd used to do. She was standing there looking very serious. In an instant Kate curbed her instinct to go and hug Rosie, sensing that the child had changed since she'd seen her last. And it *had* been a while. Rosie hadn't come to Molly's christening. Instead, when Kate reached her she just smiled and bent to kiss her formally. She pulled back and looked into dark, wary eyes, wondering what had made her so cautious.

'Rosie, you're all grown up since I last saw you. You're becoming quite the young lady.'

Kate couldn't help tucking a strand of long dark hair behind her ear. Rosie's cheeks flushed pink as she seemed to fight something, and then she mumbled an incoherent reply before turning and running back inside—presumably to her room.

Kate sensed Tiarnan behind her, sensed his impatience. 'I'm sorry about that. Rosie is going through a difficult patch. She spent time with her mother recently, which never ends well.'

Kate's heart went out to the child. She could remember her own trials and tribulations, how *her* mother hadn't wanted anything to do with the fact that her daughter was growing and developing into a young woman. She could remember the turmoil she'd felt. Maybe Rosie was going through the same thing? From what Kate could remember, Stella Rios, Rosie's mother, had never been warm.

She looked at Tiarnan. 'It's fine. You don't have to apologise.'

A buxom housekeeper bustled into the hall, and Kate tried to keep track of the rapid Spanish as Tiarnan introduced them. The woman's name was Esmerelda, and Kate greeted her warmly in Spanish. She could sense Tiarnan looking at her and turned.

'I forgot that you speak Spanish.'

Kate shrugged and coloured slightly. 'Enough to get by.'

She had spent a lot of time working in Spain some years previously, and had kept up Spanish classes when she'd returned to the US.

He regarded her for another long moment, and then gestured with an arm for her to precede him. 'We have some time before lunch is served—let me show you around.'

Kate duly followed Tiarnan through the house, her awe mounting as he revealed a sumptuously formal reception area that led into a dining room which could seat up to twenty people. But just when she was starting to feel too intimidated he drew them away, towards the other side of the house and a much more relaxed area: a comfortable sitting room, complete with overstuffed couches and shelves heaving with books, a widescreen TV, videos and DVDs on the shelves alongside it.

Something in Kate's chest clenched. This was truly a home. Warm and inviting, with colourful rugs on the exposed stone floor.

At the back of the house Tiarnan revealed an idyllic garden with sunlight glinting off an aquamarine pool set among the bushes. A slice of paradise right in the middle of one of the most cosmopolitan cities in the world.

'You have a beautiful home, Tiarnan.'

Kate said the words but they felt ineffectual, stilted. How many women had stood here and told him that?

Tiarnan was looking around them. 'Yes,' he said, almost absently.

Kate shot him a look but he was already moving, walking back towards the house. With a last lingering look at the stunning peaceful garden, Kate followed.

Tiarnan heard Kate's soft footfall behind him. Something forceful and inarticulate was rising in his chest. He'd stood outside and showed her his idyllic paradise, and yet for the first time since he'd bought it he was aware of something inherently empty about it. The image of Rosie appearing at the front door came into his mind's eye. There had been something so lonely about that image too…

He didn't know what it was that was suddenly making him so introspective. He had Kate here. He had no grand plan where she was concerned, apart from getting her into his bed. When it came to women he found it easy to detach. But right now he was feeling anything but detached. He assured himself that it was just because he knew Kate already—they had a connection. And that was why she was here. He was going to use whatever means necessary to show her that he wanted her, to get her to admit to her own desire…

Lunch was in a smaller, less formal dining room just off the huge kitchen. Esmerelda was bustling back and forth with delicious food and warm smiles, but that didn't help dissipate the slight tension in the atmosphere. Despite the fact that Tiarnan was being utterly charming and mesmeric in a way that made Kate feel extremely flustered.

Being the focus of his attention, albeit with Rosie there too, was nothing short of overwhelming. The coiled energy in his taut muscular body connected with hers and she felt jumpy. It was a monumental struggle just to try and keep up with the easy enough conversation.

Rosie was largely silent and monosyllabic when Kate tried to talk to her. Kate had realised that the faint underlying tension was between father and daughter, and she guessed it went deeper than Tiarnan had let on. Rosie was picking at her food, and when she asked in a small, ever so polite voice if she could leave the table, Tiarnan said tightly, 'You've barely said two words to Kate.'

Kate directed a quick smile at Rosie and said, 'I don't mind. She can go if she wants. I remember how boring it can be, listening to adults.'

Rosie immediately jumped up and ran out, her chair scraping on the ground as she did so, making Kate flinch slightly. Tiarnan made as if to go after her, but Kate caught his arm, jerking her hand away again when she felt the muscles bunch under the thin material of his shirt. 'Really, it's fine, Tiarnan. I don't mind.'

He sat down again and sighed heavily. 'When we moved here from the outskirts of Madrid I changed her school. It's not been the easiest of transitions, and I'm currently public enemy number one.'

Kate thought of Stella again—Tiarnan's ex-wife. She'd never really known why the marriage had ended, and Sorcha had never talked about it either, but then Tiarnan's marriage break-up and subsequent fatherhood had coincided with a hard time in Sorcha's life... Kate's attention had naturally been taken up with her friend. In all honesty she'd used every and any excuse to avoid talking or thinking about Tiarnan. And the fact that she was thinking about his marriage now irritated her intensely.

Just as that thought was highlighting the juxtaposition between how she'd always so carefully protected herself around this man and how much he'd already reeled her in, the door opened and a woman came in—someone Kate hadn't yet met. She was middle-aged, and her face was white and tense. She looked as if she'd been crying.

Tiarnan stood up. 'Paloma, this is Kate—an old friend.'

Kate stood and extended her hand. As the woman came in it was extremely obvious that she'd been crying. She shook Kate's hand and managed a distracted watery smile.

Tiarnan was looking from her to Kate. 'This is Paloma— Rosie's nanny.' Belatedly noticing Paloma's distress, he said, 'What is it? Something with Rosie?'

Kate could feel the tension spike, and guessed in an instant that Rosie had probably been giving Paloma a hard time too.

The woman shook her head and fresh tears welled,

'No, it's not Rosie, it's my son. He's been involved in an accident and he's been taken to hospital. I'm sorry, Mr Quinn, but I have to go there immediately.'

Kate put her arm around the woman's shoulders instinctively as Tiarnan quickly reassured her. 'I'll have Juan take you. Don't worry, Paloma, you'll be taken care of.'

'Thank you, Mr Quinn. I'm so sorry.'

He waved aside her apology, and with a look to Kate strode out of the room to make arrangements. Kate did her best to help out. They went to Paloma's room and Kate helped her pack.

A short while later, as they stood on the steps and watched Tiarnan's chauffeur-driven Mercedes pull away with Paloma in the back, he turned and ran a hand through his hair. 'I'm sorry, Kate. I invited you for a quiet lunch and it's been nothing but drama. I didn't intend for it to be like this.'

Kate looked up into those glittering blue eyes and felt out of her depth. Tiarnan had taken control of the situation and despatched Paloma with an assurance that she must have as much time off as she needed. She'd heard him make a call to the hospital where Paloma's son was to make sure that he was getting the best of treatment, arranging for him to be moved to a private room.

Kate knew that he would personally oversee any payment. His innate goodness and generosity made her feel vulnerable.

She shrugged a slim shoulder. 'That's OK. It couldn't be helped.'

A shadow passed over Tiarnan's face and he swore softly under his breath. He looked out past her to where the car had disappeared.

'What is it?'

He looked back to her. 'I'm due in Dublin this evening, for the AGM of the board of Sorcha's outreach programme. I promised Sorcha and Romain I'd do it for them while the baby is so small.'

'Oh…' Kate would instinctively have asked what she could do to help, but she was due on her flight back to New York herself. She knew how important Sorcha's outreach youth centre was to her. And while she'd no doubt Romain would jump on a plane to Dublin for an important meeting like this for his wife, she knew Tiarnan wouldn't want to let them down.

'Can't Esmerelda help out?'

Tiarnan shook his head. 'She's a lot older than she looks, and while she does live here, in an apartment out the back, her husband is old too and needs taking care of… I couldn't ask her to take on Rosie.'

'Your mother?' Kate knew that Mrs Quinn had moved back to her native Madrid as soon as Sorcha had left home.

'She's down in the south, staying with her sister until the spring.'

'Oh…'

'The other problem is that I'm due to fly straight to New York from Dublin tomorrow. I'm taking part in talks with a senator, the mayor and one of the major banks. It's something I couldn't get out of even if I wanted to…'

Kate's conscience pricked her. She had to say something, because she knew when she got back to New York she didn't have any work lined up. She'd told her formidable agent, Maud Harriday, that she wanted to start scaling back her work commitments, and Maud with typical brusqueness had declared that all she needed was a holiday. So now, for the first time in a long time, Kate had a few clear weeks of...nothing.

'Look, I don't have any work lined up for the next...' she stopped herself revealing too much '...the next while. I could stay here and watch Rosie if you want. I mean, if that's OK with you?'

Kate couldn't decipher the expression on Tiarnan's face. She knew he was fiercely protective of his daughter. Perhaps he didn't trust her? That thought lanced her.

'I'd enjoy having an excuse to stay in Madrid—and a chance to see Rosie properly again...'

Tiarnan looked down at Kate, taking in her clear blue gaze. She was surprising him again. Offering to take on responsibility for Rosie like this. A few lovers after his divorce had hinted at wanting to get to know Rosie, to try and become more intimate. He instinctively wanted to say no to Kate's suggestion, but found himself stopping. The immediate feeling that he could trust her with Rosie surprised him.

Kate saw him deliberate, and felt compelled to insist on helping him. She refused to investigate *that* impulse.

'Tiarnan, you're stuck. If you want to go to Dublin in two hours and New York tomorrow, who can you get to mind Rosie at such short notice? And you know if you say you can't go then Romain will have to leave Sorcha on her own with the baby.'

She was right. Tiarnan knew if Kate wasn't here, offering this solution, he would have to take Rosie with him on his trip—and that was never ideal. Especially when her routine was of paramount importance right now. And Kate wasn't some random stranger. Tiarnan knew that she'd spent time with Rosie whenever Sorcha had looked after her for him before, and his discreet security team would make sure that Rosie and she were well protected. Rosie was an independent, mature girl for her age, so she really just needed to have company. Esmerelda would be on hand too. But…

He seemed to be considering something—and then he took Kate by surprise, moving closer. She froze.

He cocked his head slightly. 'You wouldn't be doing this just to avoid me, would you, Kate? Now that you know I'm going to New York? Or even because you're hoping that this will foster some kind of longer-lasting position in my life?'

Kate clenched her fists, surprised by the strength of the hurt that rushed through her at this evidence of his cynicism, and felt anger at his arrogant assumption that her capitulation was a foregone conclusion. His mention of New York hadn't even registered—*or had it?* The evidence that she might have been faced with his relentless determination again within days sent a flare of awareness through her. She damped it down, hating that he might see something.

'No, Tiarnan. Believe it or not, I'm just trying to help.'

She saw a suspicious light flash in his eyes, as if he didn't trust her assertion. He came even closer and lifted a hand, trailing a finger over the curve of her cheekbone and down to the place where her jaw met her neck. Since when had that small area become so sensitive that she wanted to turn her face into his hand and purr like a cat?

'Good,' he said softly. 'Because I had been planning on asking you out for dinner in New York. We can discuss it when I get back.'

Suspicion slammed into Kate, clearing her lust-hazed mind as she remembered the frenetic call from Maud about this assignment, the apparent urgency. She reached up and took down Tiarnan's hand. It felt warm and strong and vital, but she forced herself to let it go and glared up at him. 'Did you have anything to do with my being sent here for this impromptu shoot?'

Tiarnan crossed his arms and looked down at Kate, completely at ease. Smug. He shrugged minutely. 'Not…exactly…'

Kate crossed her arms too, as suspicion turned into cold certainty and not a little fear at how Tiarnan was determined to manipulate her. 'What's that supposed to mean?'

His eyes turned steely. 'It means that I *might* have encouraged the CEO of the luxury brand Baudé, who is a personal friend of mine, to hire you. I was aware he was looking for a suitable model...'

Shock spread through Kate—his influence had meant that within a week of seeing him in San Francisco he had managed to get her all the way across the world to Madrid, practically gift-wrapped on his doorstep. The realisation stunned her. Evidence of his determination made her feel funny inside—confused.

'How dare you use me like that? I'm not some pawn you can just move around—'

Tiarnan took her hand, and her words halted and died.

'Kate. You know I want you. I will do whatever it takes to convince you of that and get you to admit that you want me too.'

'But...but...' Kate spluttered. The effect of him just holding her hand was sending her pulse into overdrive. 'That's positively Machiavellian.'

He came closer and lifted her hand to his mouth, pressed a kiss to the underside of her wrist. 'No. It's called desire—and it's a desire I've denied for a long, long time...'

Ten years. It hung there between them like an accusation.

'Tiarnan,' Kate said weakly. 'It was so long ago...it was just a kiss...we're not the same...'

'So why does it feel like it was only yesterday, and that it was more than just a kiss?'

And right then, with Tiarnan holding her hand and standing so close, it slammed back into Kate with all the intensity as if it had been yesterday. It was exactly the same for her. The only problem was it had never diminished for her, while he'd been busy getting married, having a baby. Forgetting her. Until now. Because he was bored, or intrigued to know what he'd refused?

Kate tried to pull her hand away, but he was remorseless, wouldn't let go. She glared up at him, feeling panic rise, feeling inarticulate.

Tiarnan's voice was eminently reasonable. 'I may have suggested you to someone for a campaign. That's all I did. I wanted to meet you here, show you that I meant what I said in San Francisco…and then in New York I was hoping that you'd agree to go out with me. Give us a chance.' He grimaced. 'What happened with Paloma today was out of even *my* control.'

Kate flushed and looked down for a moment. The panic was still there, but she fought it down. 'Of course it is. You couldn't have known that would happen.'

She looked up then, and finally managed to pull her hand from his. She stepped back to give herself space. But she knew it was useless. Tiarnan Quinn was fast filling every space within her and around her—as only he could.

'Look, I'm offering to stay and watch Rosie till you get back. Apart from that…' She shook her head. 'I—'

Tiarnan put a finger to Kate's mouth. 'Just…think about it, OK?'

Kate looked into his eyes for a long moment, and what she saw there alternately scared the life out of her and made her want to wrap her arms around his neck and have him kiss her— exactly as she'd been wanting him to since the christening in France. Eventually, feeling weak, she nodded. It was only a small movement, but it seemed that Tiarnan was happy enough with that. She was afraid he'd seen some capitulation in her eyes that she wasn't even aware of.

'Good. And thank you for offering to stay.' He stepped back too, and gestured for her to precede him back into the house. 'I'd better see if Rosie's OK with this, and fill you in on all the details of her routine.'

Kate walked back into the house and felt as if she was stepping over a line in the sand. She just hoped and prayed that someone would come along and divert Tiarnan's attention in New York. And yet as soon as she had that thought the acid bile of jealousy rose. Kate was very afraid that when Tiarnan returned she wouldn't have the strength to resist him…

Kate's eyes were tired. She put down what she was working on and sat back in the couch for a moment, closing her eyes, pinching the bridge of her nose. She was waiting up for Tiarnan. He was due home at any time now. He'd been gone for three days.

Kate was all geared up to be clear and firm. She fully intended flying back to New York first thing in the morning. The thought of Rosie, though, made her heart clench. It had taken some time—a couple of days of Kate walking her to and from her new school nearby, chatting easily about this and that—for a sense of the familiar old accord to come back. And while it wasn't exactly the way it had been, things were definitely thawing. Rosie clearly had a lot going on in her serious little head.

Earlier that evening, after Kate had bent down to kiss her goodnight, she'd been surprised and touched when a pair of skinny arms had crept around her neck and held on tight for a second. Rosie had said nothing, and Kate hadn't pushed it, just crept out of the room, her heart swelling with emotion. Emotion she shouldn't be allowing herself to feel for the little girl. *Or* her father.

Kate was surprised to admit to herself that in the past few days she'd felt an increasing sense of relaxation stealing over her. It had been so long since she'd slowed her pace. Stopping at the local café on her way home from seeing Rosie off to school each day, taking time to just read the paper had reminded her of how long it had been since she'd devoted any time to herself.

Sorcha had phoned earlier, and Kate hadn't missed the open curiosity in her voice. Kate hated misleading her friend, keeping the real nature of what was going on with Tiarnan from her, but Sorcha was just too close, so she'd passed off the chain of events that had led her to Madrid as just coincidence. But it was no coincidence that she was sitting curled up on Tiarnan's couch, waiting for him to come home, and no coincidence that was causing this churning mixture of excitement and turmoil in her belly…

Tiarnan stood at the door of the living room. The house was silent, warm. A sense of peace washed over him—the same peace he always felt when he got home and checked that Rosie was safe, tucked up in bed asleep. And yet tonight, after checking on her, that quality of peace was deeper, more profound.

One dim lamp was lit and on the couch was the curled-up figure of a woman. Kate. Here in his house. *His.* Satisfaction coursed through him. He walked in, the rug muffling his steps. She was asleep, hair tumbled over one shoulder in a bright coil of white-gold. His eyes travelled over her lissom form—what he could see of it in faded jeans and plaid button-down shirt. Her feet were bare, delicately arched, toenails painted with clear gloss. Desire was instant and burning within him.

He shrugged off his jacket and threw it onto the edge of the couch, sitting down beside Kate. She moved slightly in her sleep, sliding towards him, towards the depression he'd made. Tiarnan put an arm across the back of the couch and leant towards her face, which was turned towards him.

'Kate,' he whispered softly. She didn't stir.

He'd never been turned on by sleeping women, usually preferring them awake and willing, but there was something so perfect about Kate in sleep, her cheeks flushed a slight pink, her mouth in a little *moue,* that he couldn't resist the temptation to bend even closer and press his mouth to hers.

Kate knew she was dreaming, but it was too delicious a dream to wake herself from just yet. A man's mouth was moving over hers enticingly, softly, as if coaxing a response.

And, as if watching herself from outside her own body, she gave full rein to her imagination and let it be Tiarnan; let it be *his* hard, sensual mouth. It felt so good, so right, and on a sigh that seemed to draw in pure lust she opened her mouth against his.

She felt his deep moan of approval. It rumbled through her whole body, sensitising every point, making her breasts tighten, the tips harden into points. When his tongue sought entry to explore and tease, she smiled against his lips, her own tongue making a bold foray, tasting his, sucking it deep. She arched her body, wanting to feel more…

On some level, even while Kate knew she was dreaming, she was also very aware of the fact that she was in Madrid, in Tiarnan's house, waiting up for him to come home from the US… As if she'd climbed too high in consciousness to stay where she'd been, the shocking realisation came that she was no longer dreaming…what was happening was very real. *Tiarnan!*

Kate's eyes flew open, and at the same time she became aware of her heart racing and her breath coming hard and fast. She also became aware of slumberous blue eyes looking directly into hers. As if he'd sensed her wakefulness before she did, Tiarnan had moved back slightly. Her hands were on his shoulders, *clutching them to her,* not in the act of pushing him away. Her mouth felt bruised, sensitive. She remembered the hunger of that kiss just now. And yet amongst the shock and dismay that splintered her brain was pure joy at seeing him again.

It was all too much for her to process for a minute, seeing him here like this. She reacted against that feeling of joy and tried to push him away with all her might.

'What do you think you're *doing?*'

She gave another huge push, but Tiarnan was like a rock and still far too close. His mouth quirked sexily and everything seemed to slam into Kate at once: the dimness of the room, his scent, his body so close to hers. *Her wanton reaction.*

'Waking you with a kiss.'

She reacted violently to his voice, feeling acutely vulnerable—he'd taken deliberate advantage of her, and the more he did it, the less she could argue to him or herself that she was immune to him. If he knew how close this was to the fantasy she'd had for a long time…

She pushed again, feeling heat rise in her face. 'Finding me asleep did *not* give you the right to molest me.'

Tiarnan finally rolled back and away, releasing her, but a mocking look on his face cut right through her flimsy attack.

'Kate, believe me, I wasn't— *What the—?*' He suddenly jumped up like a scalded cat, holding something in his hand.

Kate immediately saw what it was.

'What the hell is that?' Genuine pain throbbed in his voice, and Kate allowed herself a small dart of pleasure; that would teach him.

She stood up and took the offending article from him. 'It's a knitting needle.' She indicated the couch and the pile of knitting that had rolled off her lap when she'd fallen asleep. 'I'm knitting a jumper for Molly, for Christmas.'

His mouth opened and closed. Kate saw a genuine lack of comprehension in his eyes, and then she looked down to where his hand still held his side, just above his trousers. A dark shape was flowering outwards through a small rip in his shirt, under his hand.

Shock slammed into Kate, turning her cold in a second. 'Tiarnan—you're *bleeding*.'

His mouth was a tight line. 'It went right into me.'

Acting on pure instinct, and feeling a shard of fear rush through her, Kate reached out and ripped open the bottom of his shirt. The wound was a small puncture, but it was pumping blood, and when she looked up at Tiarnan he'd gone white. Too panicked to feel bemused at his obvious distaste for blood, Kate held his shirt to the wound and led him out to the kitchen, where she found the first aid kit under the sink.

She made him rest back on the huge wooden table as she opened his shirt all the way to tend to him. She felt shaky. 'I'm so sorry, Tiarnan. I'd no idea you were leaning on the needle…'

He just grunted, and Kate busied herself stanching the blood. She applied pressure to a piece of cotton wool over the wound for a long moment, and looked at him warily. Colour had come back into his cheeks and his eyes were now glittering into hers.

He arched an incredulous brow. 'Knitting?'

She smiled weakly. 'It's a hobby. Something I took up to pass the time backstage at the shows.'

'Reading would have been too boring, I take it?' His tone was as dry as toast.

She smiled again. 'And smash the stereotype that all models are thick?'

A glint of humour passed between them, and suddenly Kate became very aware of the fact that Tiarnan was lounging back, lean hips resting on the table, shirt open, impressive chest bare. In a surge of awareness, now that the panic was gone, she unthinkingly applied more pressure, making Tiarnan wince.

'Sorry,' she muttered, lifting the cotton wool to check if the bleeding had stopped. To her relief it had, and it didn't look as if the needle had gone too deep. But now all she could think about was the fact that she was right between his splayed legs. The material of his trousers was pulled taut over firmly muscled thighs. His belt buckle glinted and a line of dark silken hair led upwards over a hard flat belly, like an enticement to his chest, which was covered with more dark hair. She had a sudden burning desire to know what it would be like to have her bare breasts pressed against his chest…

She grew hot again as she busied herself cleaning the wound and getting a plaster to hold it in place. Her hands didn't feel steady, and she prayed that Tiarnan wasn't noticing her meltdown.

What Tiarnan *was* noticing was the tantalising display of her breasts, just visible as she moved, in the vee of her shirt. From what he could see she wore a plain white bra, and her breasts looked soft and voluptuous. Perfectly shaped. He could remember how they'd felt, crushed against his chest. Her soft, evocative scent wafted up from her body as she moved. Her legs looked impossibly long in the faded jeans. He shifted on the table as she bent down and unwittingly came closer to where he was starting to ache unmercifully. The pain of where the needle had lanced him faded in comparison. The incongruity of finding that she'd been knitting in the first place—not a hobby that he associated with a woman like her—had faded too, in the heat of his arousal.

If she looked down... He gritted his teeth, trying to control his body, a muscle throbbing in his jaw as her soft small hands worked. Her hair slid over her shoulder then, and whispered against his belly. Everything in him tightened, and he couldn't help a groan. Immediately Kate looked up with wide, innocent eyes, inflaming him even more.

'Did I hurt you?' He shook his head. She was finished putting on the plaster. He could hear the tremor in her voice when she said, 'There—all done.'

He reached out and held her elbows, dragging her imperceptibly closer, and closed his legs around hers slightly. He could see her widening eyes, pupils enlarging, and it had a direct effect on his arousal levels. She was tantalisingly close to where his erection strained against his trousers. But not close enough.

His voice felt as if it was being dragged over gravel. 'Not all done yet... I think you should kiss it better.'

Kate's insides seemed to be melting and combusting all at once. She was unable to look away from Tiarnan's gaze. It held her like a magnet. Time stood still around them. She was so close now. One little tiny step and she'd be right there, captive between his legs, and she would be able to feel... She had to stop this madness. She had to remember that he'd deliberately set out to get her to Madrid to seduce her—had to remember her vow to be strong, resolute. She *couldn't* let this happen. She struggled to swallow.

'Tiarnan, you're not four years old…' Her voice sounded pathetically weak and feeble.

'You stabbed me with your knitting needle,' he growled. 'The least you can do is kiss me better.'

What they were saying should have had a thread of easy humour. But humour was long gone. This was deadly serious.

Kate's heart was pumping so fast now she felt sure he would be able to hear it. His hands on her elbows were strong, rigid. He wasn't going to let her go, and she didn't even know if she would have the strength to step away without falling down. This was the most erotically charged moment she could ever remember experiencing. Her throat was as dry as sandpaper.

'One kiss and then you'll let me go?'

Without taking his eyes from hers, he nodded.

Kate pulled away slightly and Tiarnan let go—cautiously. He leant back a little farther and rested his hands behind him on the table. It made him appear vulnerable and even more sexy, his torso long and lean, shoulders broad. Kate looked down at where the wound was. She put her hands behind her back, as if she couldn't trust herself not to run her fingers over the ridges of muscles that rippled over his belly. She felt weak inside—hot and achy.

She bent down over his chest, and down further, her mouth hovering over where the plaster was. His skin was dark olive, taut and gleaming, begging to be touched, kissed. She imagined it to be hot to the touch, and pressed her mouth just above the plaster. Without having consciously intended it, her mouth was slightly open. She could feel and hear his indrawn breath. Acting on pure instinct, Kate darted her tongue-tip out for the tiniest moment. His skin was warm, and slightly salty on her tongue. Lust coiled through her like a live flame. She could smell the musk of arousal and didn't know if it was hers or his.

She wanted with a desperate urgency to explore further, to press herself close and feel if he was aroused…

With every atom of strength Kate possessed, she managed to straighten up and look Tiarnan in the eye. Her hands were still clenched tight behind her back. She felt feverish. His eyes burned into hers, and suddenly Tiarnan's hands gripped her upper arms and he pulled her right into him. Caught off balance, she fell forward. He caught her full weight, and her hands came out automatically to splay across his chest. Desire flooded her belly and between her legs with traitorous urgency.

'Your wound…' she gasped.

'Will be fine.'

She was desperate now. As desperate for him to keep holding her as she was to get away—and that killed her. 'You said one kiss.'

He looked at her for a long moment. Kate felt her breasts crushed to his chest and, worse, felt his arousal hard against the apex of her legs. She was right in the cradle of his lap, unable to save herself from falling headlong into the fire. Her whole body was crying out to mould into his, to allow it to go up in flames.

She repeated herself, as if that might change the direction things had been taking since he'd walked up to her on that stage in San Francisco.

'You said one kiss.'

Tiarnan snaked one arm around her back, pulling her in even tighter. The other went to the back of her head. She was his captive, and she couldn't move even if she wanted to.

'I lied.'

CHAPTER FOUR

TIARNAN'S mouth came down onto Kate's with all the devastation of a match being put to a dry piece of tinder. Ten years of build-up exploded inside her. Her hands curled into his chest and he pulled her so close to his body that all she could feel was rock-hard muscle and his arousal. Kate could feel moisture gather between her legs and she moved unconsciously, as if she could assuage the need building there.

With a move she wasn't even aware of Tiarnan shifted them, so that Kate was now sitting on the table and he was leaning over her. Eyes closed, Kate could only feel and experience, and give herself up to the onslaught on her senses. Tiarnan's hands were in her hair, around her face. His mouth was relentless, not breaking contact, his tongue stabbing deep—and she was as insatiable as he.

Her arms wound up around his neck, clinging, hands tangling in his short silky hair. She finally broke her mouth away for a brief moment, sucking in harsh breaths. Her heart hammered as she felt Tiarnan's hands move down, moulding over her waist, cupping under her buttocks, pulling her into him even more.

She opened her eyes, but they felt heavy, Tiarnan's face was close, his breath feathering across her face, his mouth hovering. Feeling bereft, Kate reached up again and pressed her mouth feverishly to his, her whole body arching into Tiarnan's, revelling in his hard strength. No other man had ever made her feel so hot, so sensual.

Tiarnan's hands went to her shirt and she could feel him open the buttons, fingers grazing her skin, the curve of her breasts. She didn't protest—she couldn't. Impatient to touch him too, she pushed his shirt off completely, so his chest was bare, and ran her hands over the smooth skin of his shoulders. She felt the muscles move under his skin as his hands pushed aside her shirt. His mouth left hers and blazed a trail of kisses down over her jaw and neck. Kate's head fell back. All she was aware of was here and now and how badly she craved this touch. *His* touch.

Tiarnan's arm supported her as he tipped her off balance slightly so she leant further back. His mouth was on the upper slope of her breast and all her nerve-endings seemed to have gathered at the tip, so tight it hurt.

When she felt him pull down her bra strap and then her bra to expose her breast, her breath stopped. Tiarnan cupped the voluptuous mound with one hand, his thumb passing back and forth over the hard aching tip. Kate bit her lip and looked down. She was breathing fast, one hand behind her, trying to balance, clenched into the table as if that could stop her tipping over the edge of this sensation. Between her legs she burned, and she could feel herself fighting the urge to push into Tiarnan's body.

'So beautiful...' he breathed, looking down at her cupped breast with its pouting dusky peak.

Before Kate could gather her fractured thoughts and steady her breathing he lowered his head and his mouth closed over her nipple. She let out a long moan somewhere between torture and heaven as he drew it into the hot cavern of his mouth and suckled.

This felt so right—as if they had been transported back in time and this was a natural progression of that kiss. And yet...it shouldn't be. Not after ten years. How could ten years of other experiences be obliterated so easily? Wiped out as if they hadn't even existed?

It was that tiny sliver of rationality seeping into her head that woke Kate from her sensual trance. She became aware of the fact that she was practically supine on the kitchen table, and when she felt Tiarnan's hand search for and find the button on her jeans, about to flick it open, she struggled upwards, battling a fierce desire to just give in.

'No…*no,* Tiarnan. *Stop.*' Her hands were on his arms, pushing him back.

After a long moment he stood up, chest heaving, cheeks flushed, eyes glittering. Kate knew she wasn't much more composed. She dropped her hands. Her voice felt raw.

'We can't do this. Rosie might wake and find us…or Esmerelda.'

He looked at her for a long moment and finally took a step back, raking a hand through his short hair. He emanated veritable waves of danger, his face stark with a raw masculine beauty that nearly made Kate throw herself back into his arms. But she didn't.

She stood from the table on shaky legs and pulled her bra up, her shirt together, turning her back to him for a moment. She felt dizzy.

His voice cut through her dizziness. 'A few moments more and here would have done fine… But you're right. This isn't the time or the place.'

She rejected the almost violent need that beat through her body. She knew he was right; a few more moments and here *would* have been fine. Anywhere would have been fine. *The rug in front of the fire.* Any feeling of exhilaration that their desire had been mutual was lost in the humiliation that burned her again. Her voice was fierce.

'There won't *be* a time or place, Tiarnan.'

Kate felt a hard hand on her arm and she was pulled around to face him. His face was glowering down at her, taut with a frustrated need that had to be reflected on hers too.

'How can you deny what just happened here?'

Tiarnan saw Kate's eyes widen and he let her go. The force of need running through him was so strong he was actually afraid he couldn't contain it. She'd felt like nothing he could describe or articulate in his arms. Soft and fragrant and pliant…and so passionate. But he was shocked to come to his senses and acknowledge that if she hadn't stopped him he would be taking her right now on the kitchen table, overhead lights blazing down, like some overgrown teenager who couldn't wait.

Where was his sophistication? His cool logical approach to such matters? *She'd* had to remind *him* about Rosie. She stood, holding her shirt together, hair tousled over her shoulders, her cheeks flushed, lips red and engorged with blood. His hormones were already raging back to life. He had to get a grip.

Kate struggled to close her shirt. She felt as though she'd just been through some kind of seismic earth shift. She watched as Tiarnan's face closed down. He bent to pick up his shirt, muscles rippling across his back, and when he put it on her eye was drawn to the rip and the dark stain of blood. Her belly clenched. She couldn't answer his words. Couldn't deny what had happened.

She looked down, struggling with her bottom button, feeling tears threaten. *God.* How could she have been so unutterably weak?

'Kate.'

She composed herself and finally closed the button before looking up. She hoped her face was blank, her eyes giving nothing away. She couldn't count on her years of training around Tiarnan any more. Her control was shot to pieces.

His shirt was back on, haphazardly done up, making Kate's heart turn over and making her want to do it up properly for him. She clenched her hands by her sides, fought the urge to tidy her hair, which was all over the place.

His eyes snared hers. She couldn't look away. Her mind blanked.

'I never meant to leap on you the minute I walked in the door…but you can see what happens between us…'

'I—'

His face tightened. '*Don't* deny it, Kate. At least don't do that.'

Kate shut her mouth. She hadn't been sure what she was going to say, but he was right. She'd been about to try and make some excuse for what had happened.

Tiarnan turned away and paced for a moment, before coming back to stand right in front of her. He looked grim. 'I was going to ask you tomorrow, but it seems as if now is as good a time as any.'

'Ask me what…?' Kate said nervously.

'Rosie's school is giving them some holidays from the day after tomorrow while they do some unavoidable renovation work. We're going to our house in Martinique. I'd like you to come with us.'

Kate could feel herself pale. She took a step back and started shaking her head, her heart beating fast.

Tiarnan watched her. 'You know why I'm asking you, Kate. You know what will happen if you say yes. But know this—if you say no, if you insist on returning to New York tomorrow, it won't change anything… I'm not letting you go. Not when we have unfinished business between us. Not when we have *this*.'

He reached out a hand and cupped her cheek. Immediate heat suffused her whole body and electricity made the air between them crackle. He was determined. Nevertheless, she had to hang onto some control. She pulled down his hand and stepped back.

'I need to leave here by eleven to catch my flight. I'd appreciate it if you could call a cab for me in the morning.'

Kate saw Tiarnan's jaw clench, but he just said, 'You won't need a cab. I'll take you if you want to go. *If* you want to go.'

'I will—'

Tiarnan cut her off, changed tack, and surprised himself when he said, 'When I went in to check on Rosie earlier she looked more peaceful than she's done in weeks.'

Kate shook her head, her heart constricting. 'Tiarnan, don't do this.'

Surprise at that admission, and at the way Kate was reacting, made him sound harsh. 'Look, you did me a huge favour minding Rosie. You've got time off, and you probably haven't had a holiday in months…'

Years, she said in her head, and right now it felt as if she'd been running from something for years. That sense of peace that had been stealing over her these last couple of days was elusively seductive, but there was no way she would relax around this man.

'I *would* like you to come on holiday with us. I spoke to Rosie on the phone about it earlier, and she said she'd love to have you come. I asked her not to say anything until I'd spoken to you… Just sleep on it, OK? And let me know in the morning.'

His tone brooked no argument. Pure arrogance. Kate felt tense.

'Fine. Tell yourself what you want. I know what I'll be doing tomorrow.'

Escaping from you again.

Kate backed away while she could and turned away. And felt as if she were being hounded by jeering voices all the way to her room.

Tiarnan watched the space Kate had left for a long moment. She'd rapidly taken up a place in his life he wasn't used to women occupying. He'd already drawn her into an intimate space that no other woman had occupied just by inviting her here, by letting her take care of Rosie. Apart from family, his wife was the only other woman who'd been that close; familiar darkness filled his chest. *She* didn't count.

And even his wife had never taken such control of his every waking and sleeping thought as Kate was beginning to. He tried to rationalise that moment in New York when in the middle of an important meeting his mind had wandered helplessly and he'd had the lightbulb inspiration of asking Kate to join them on holiday. How right it had felt.

He'd tried to tell himself that it was for Rosie as much as himself; he was becoming more and more acutely aware, as she grew older, of the lack of a solid female role model in her life. Yet he'd never introduce anyone into their intimate circle who Rosie wasn't completely comfortable with. When he'd mentioned asking Kate along on holiday to Rosie she'd been more excited about the prospect than she'd been about anything in weeks. The fact that they'd obviously bonded merely comforted him that he'd made the right decision. And he *did* genuinely feel grateful to Kate for stepping in to care for Rosie at such short notice. But he knew that for all his high-minded intentions a much baser desire lay behind the sudden impetus to ask her to come. He just wanted her in one place: in his bed, underneath him.

He recalled her obvious shock at the suggestion and felt curiously vulnerable before he quashed it ruthlessly. He had to wonder if this playing hard to get was just a game. Punishment for his earlier rejection? Or foreplay because she knew she was going to give in? A stab of disappointment ran through him; he didn't want that, but couldn't articulate why he couldn't accept that calculated behaviour from her when he might expect it from another woman. Conflicting emotions rose up, muddying the clarity of his thought, his intention.

One thing was clear: he wanted to keep Kate close until such time as he could let her go again, and he knew that day would come. He couldn't fathom any woman ever taking up that much space *for ever.* He'd never felt that way about anyone.

His conscience pricked. There had been one moment—that night ten years ago, when Kate had all but admitted she was a virgin. The realisation had tapped into something within him and he'd felt compelled to pull back, push her away. He'd found himself reacting from a place of shock—shock at how immediate and raw his response had been. And he'd been more curt than he had intended. The flare of wounded emotion in her eyes had seared through him, but after a moment it had been as if he'd imagined it.

And then her cool response had been all the proof he'd needed that she was exactly the same as every other woman. That momentary weakness he'd felt had been a lesson learnt— a lesson he'd needed in those months afterwards when he'd dealt with his duplicitous wife. If anything, what he'd experienced with Kate and subsequently with Stella had merely re-inforced his own cynical belief system.

No, all he and Kate had was history—unfinished business. Thinking of how much he wanted her made him feel ruthless, and he never usually felt ruthless when it came to women. They didn't arouse such passionate feelings. Grim determination filled him as he refused to look any deeper into those feelings. Bed Kate and get her out of his system. There was nothing more to it than that. And if she said yes tomorrow she'd only be proving to him that all this was a playful front. And that was fine. It was all he wanted—wasn't it?

Kate lay on her back as the pre-dawn light stole into her bedroom, a tight knot low in her belly. She'd tossed and turned all night. And now she lay gritty-eyed, staring up at the ceiling.

Turmoil couldn't even begin to describe what she'd been going through in the wee small hours. As if she even had to *think* about Tiarnan's offer: of *course* she would not be going with him to some tropical island paradise to indulge in an affair. Yet, instead of feeling at peace with her decision, she was back in time and standing before Tiarnan in that library, with nothing but the firelight illuminating the room.

At the age of eighteen Kate, despite the fact that she'd been modelling on the international circuit for a couple of years and living in London, had still been unbelievably gauche and unsure of herself. But she'd learnt the art of projecting a cool, dignified façade from an early age, and she used it like an armour.

Kate had accepted Sorcha's plea to come and spend Christmas with her and her mother in Dublin; her own mother had been on holiday with a new husband. When Tiarnan had shown up unexpectedly for the family Christmas party, Kate's world had instantly imploded. She'd been in awe of him since he'd dropped her and Sorcha off at school one Sunday evening in his snazzy sports car. *All* the other girls in the boarding school had swooned that day. But Kate, as Sorcha's friend, had got to see a lot more of Tiarnan than the others. And as the years had progressed she'd developed a crush of monumental proportions.

The night of that party, after only seeing him fleetingly at his father's funeral some months before, and not for quite a while before that, to her he'd become even more handsome, more charismatic, with that cynical edge he still possessed today. Kate had been wearing a dress borrowed from Sorcha, far too tight and short for her liking, and had spent the evening avoiding Tiarnan's penetrating speculative gaze, trying to pull the dress down to cover her thighs. Feeling utterly over-whelmed, and not a little dismayed at her reaction to seeing him again when she'd hoped she would have grown out of such feelings, Kate had slipped away to try and compose herself.

She'd gone into the library, ran smack-bang into Tiarnan, and all good intentions had disappeared instantly. Her crush had solidified there and then into pure grown-up lust. But then something amazing had happened. Alone in that darkened room…looking into his eyes…she'd sensed instinctively that he was looking at her for the first time as an adult. She'd seen it in the quality of his gaze when he'd arrived to the party—it was what had made her feel so self-conscious.

Realising this had been headier than the most potent drink.

An electric awareness had sprung to life between them and she'd experienced a feeling of confidence for the first time in her life. A heady *female* confidence. The kind of confidence she faked for photographers and on the catwalk every day. She was tired of faking it. She wanted to *know* it. And she'd known that the only man who could teach her—who she *wanted* to teach her—was standing right in front of her. She'd known if she didn't seize the moment then, she never would. With that brand-new confidence something reckless had gripped her, and she'd stepped up to Tiarnan and boldly told him she wanted him. And then she'd kissed him.

Kate cringed now in the bed, ten years later, as it all flooded back. To have Tiarnan respond to her untutored kisses had been the most potent aphrodisiac. He'd pulled her close and she'd gone up in flames, pressing herself even closer to him. It had only been when his hand had found the hem of her dress and started to pull it up that reality had intruded for a rude moment. She'd instinctively frozen, becoming acutely aware of her lack of experience and the fact that a very aroused Tiarnan Quinn was about to make love to her. In an instant he'd pulled back and put her away from him with hard hands on her shoulders, looking down at her with glittering angry eyes.

Her heart thudded. So much had happened that night. Whatever romantic notions she might have entertained for a brief moment had been ruthlessly ripped apart within minutes.

She'd looked down, mortified and he'd ruthlessly tipped up her chin and asked brutally, 'Kate, are you a virgin?'

The flare of colour she had felt rising in her cheeks had told him her answer as eloquently as speaking it out loud. He'd spun away towards the fire, turning his back to her for a long moment. Their breathing had been harsh in the quiet room. She could remember how loudly her heart had been beating.

In that moment while he'd turned away Kate had struggled

to claw back some composure. Some semblance of dignity. The fact that he was rejecting her was blatantly obvious.

He'd finally turned back to face her, tall and proud, every line in his body rigid. Kate had forced herself to face him, and the coldly speculative gleam tinged with concern in his eyes had been an instant master class in making her realise just how naïve she'd been.

And then he'd said, 'Kate—look. I'm not sure what just happened—*hell.*' He'd run a hand through his hair and his expletive had made her flinch. His eyes had speared her again. 'I don't sleep with friends of my sister. You're just a kid, Kate, what the hell were you thinking?'

Tears had pricked behind Kate's eyes at the unfairness of that statement. Until just moments ago he'd been with her all the way… And then for an awful moment she doubted that it had even happened the way she'd thought. Had he in fact been trying to push her away all along, and she'd been so ardent she hadn't even noticed? A sensation of excruciating vulnerability had crawled up her spine and she'd called on every single bit of training she possessed. All the years of her mother instructing her not to show emotion, to be pretty and placid.

'Look, Tiarnan, it's no big deal. I just wanted…'

She'd racked her shocked and malfunctioning brain for something to say—something to make it seem as if she didn't care. As if kissing him hadn't been the single most cataclysmic thing that had ever happened to her. Because he was Tiarnan Quinn, and he didn't *do* tender kissing scenes with his little sister's best friend and she should have realised that…

She repeated her words and shrugged. 'I just wanted to kiss you.' She felt exposed and numb. Cold. 'I wanted to lose my virginity, and you…well, I know you, and it seemed—'

Tiarnan had jerked back as if shot, staring down at her with eyes as cold as ice. 'What? As if I'd do because I was handy and available? You don't pull your punches, Kate…'

His face was stonily impenetrable. 'Do you know, it's funny,' he said, almost to himself. 'I might have actually assumed for a moment that you were different…' He shook his head. 'But women never cease to amaze me. Even an innocent like you.'

He'd come close, making a violent tremor go through her whole body, before he'd casually picked up his dinner jacket from where *she* had pushed it off his shoulders onto the floor. His voice had been so cold it had made her shiver, her hands clench tight.

'Go and find yourself a boy your own age, Kate. He'll be much more gentle and understanding than I ever could be.'

And then he'd cupped her chin with his big hand, forcing her gaze upwards to his. She'd gritted her jaw against his fingers.

'And when you've finished with him, go easy on the others…you're undoubtedly a consummate seductress in the making. I've already met the mature version of the woman you'll undoubtedly become.'

And within a scant week of that soul-destroying little speech, before Kate had had time to gather the tattered shreds of her dignity, news had broken of Tiarnan's impending parenthood with his South American ex-girlfriend. Rumours had abounded of upcoming nuptials, which had shortly afterwards been confirmed. Evidently his most recent association with the dark beauty Stella Rios had resulted in more than a kiss goodbye. And, even more evidently, renowned playboy and bachelor Tiarnan Quinn was happy to settle down overnight and avoid the clumsy moves of a woman *like her.*

Kate sighed. Raking up the past was no help, but the memories were still so fresh, the hurt still like a deep raw wound. That night she'd attempted to play with fire and had been badly burnt. She'd been shocked at how deeply Tiarnan's cynicism had run. His easy cruelty had dea her a harsh first lesson in allowing herself to be vulnerable. And the fact that he'd read her so wrong had hurt more than she could say.

When would she *ever* be free of his hold over her? Especially now that he'd made it obvious he still desired her? At least before she hadn't had to contend with being the target of Tiarnan's attention…and she knew how determined he could be. He hadn't made his fortune and become one of the most influential men in the world through lack of determination. Now that he knew her weakness for him he would pursue her with single-mindedness until she gave in. Until she was powerless before him.

A flutter of traitorous excitement snuck into her belly, cancelling out the knot of tension even as Kate tried to reject the accompanying thought—a mere dark whisper of a suggestion: *What if she gave in?* She immediately rejected the audacious thought outright, aghast that her sense of pride had even let it surface.

But it wouldn't go, staying and growing bigger in her mind with obstinate persistence. And with it came an awful feeling of rightness, of inevitability. A surge of desire flared in the pit of her belly, between her legs, all the stronger because she'd been so desperately suppressing it.

But what if she looked at it as Tiarnan was so obviously looking at it? He had no idea she'd never really got over that night—had no idea and never *would* know that he'd hurt her so deeply. He had no idea that she'd all but believed herself to have become frigid. And he had no idea that last night had proved to her that she wasn't frigid; she was just inexplicably bound to one man. *Him.* A playboy who could never give her the stability she needed, who would undoubtedly hurt her all over again.

Kate clenched her fists, a sense of anger rising at his implicit power over her. Maybe she needed to play him at his own game? Perhaps the only way she could ever truly get over Tiarnan would be to give in? Allow this seduction. Render his hold over her impotent by sating her desire. It had to be because that kiss that night had assumed mythical proportions in her head. Despite her reaction to him just last night, who was to say if it went further he wouldn't have exactly the same effect as every other man had had? Ultimately one of disappointment.

If she slept with him—if she got him out of her system and negated his hold over her, restored the balance of his initial rejection—perhaps then she could walk away, not look back, and find the peace and happiness she craved in her life. Find someone to love, settle down with.

She'd had a fantasy vision of the life she wanted to create for herself ever since she'd been a small girl and had realised that her mother loved herself far more than she loved her, and that her father cared only about his work—to the point where it eventually killed him prematurely. Her life would be as far from her emotionally barren childhood as she could get, and while she knew that a man like Tiarnan Quinn was never going to play the starring role in that scenario, was this in fact an opportunity to gain closure? His words last night came back to her: *Unfinished business.* Wasn't that all he was to her too?

For the first time all night, as dawn broke in earnest outside, Kate felt peace steal over her like a complicit traitor.

'Are you going to tell me what's *really* going on?

Kate sat down heavily on her bed and bit her lip. Her knuckles were white around the mobile phone she held to her ear. Her open suitcase, half packed on the floor, said it all, and she didn't have to look at the clock to know she'd already missed her flight to New York.

She closed her eyes. 'Tiarnan's invited me to go to Martinique with him and Rosie for a holiday, and I've said yes.'

'Yes, I know that, Kate.'

Kate's belly felt queasy. Sorcha *never* called her Kate unless she was upset.

Her friend continued. 'I've just been talking to Tiarnan, and—oh, I don't know—a few things aren't exactly adding up: like the fact that little more than a week ago my brother paid a fortune to kiss you in front of hundreds of people when he avoided a public display of affection even on his wedding day; like you're still in his house in Madrid and tomorrow you're heading to a tropical paradise together.'

'With Rosie too,' Kate quickly asserted—as if that could save her now.

'Kate Lancaster, please give me some credit.'

The hurt in her friend's voice was unmistakable, and Kate's heart clenched painfully.

'Don't you think it's always been glaringly obvious to me that you're never exactly overjoyed when Tiarnan is around? You close up tighter than an oyster protecting a pearl.' Sorcha's voice changed then, became more gentle. 'Look, I know something happened between you two all those years ago in Dublin.'

Kate could feel the colour drain from her face. 'Sorcha, I—'

Sorcha sighed audibly. 'It's OK, you don't have to say anything. I just knew…and when you never said anything I didn't want to push it. But I just… Katie, you were there for me when I needed you, and I always wished that you'd trusted me enough to be there for you too.'

Kate's stomach had plummeted to the ground. 'Sorch, I'm so sorry. I *do* trust you—of course I do… I just—he's your brother, and I was just so mortified. It wasn't that I didn't trust you…'

'OK, look, we can talk about it again—but right now just tell me: do you know what you're doing?'

What could Kate say? She felt a bubble of hysteria rise. She was lurching between excoriating confusion and being absolutely sure that this was what she should be doing every two seconds. When she'd gone down to see Tiarnan in his study, after he'd come home from dropping Rosie to school, all rationality had flown out of the window. Yet despite her early-morning revelations, she'd been so determined to resist the awful temptation to give in and bring to life her greatest fantasy.

He'd stood from behind his desk, tall and intimidating, and

so gorgeous that her mouth had dried up. Like watching a car crash in slow motion, she'd heard herself blurting out, 'You said that night that you don't sleep with your sister's friends—so what's changed?'

Instantly she'd cringed at how she'd given herself away so spectacularly, proving that she remembered every word he'd said.

Tiarnan had come around the desk slowly, to stand lethally close. His eyes so blue it had nearly hurt to look at him.

'Everything. You're no longer an innocent eighteen-year-old. You've matured into a beautiful woman and the boundaries I would have respected before around your friendship with my sister have changed too. She's married, getting on with her own life... Don't you want to do the same, Kate? Haven't you always wondered what it would be like?'

Hurt lanced her at his uncanny ability to strike at the very heart of her most vulnerable self. And the fact that what he said underlined the biggest understatement of her life had rankled unbearably.

'So I'm good enough to take to bed now, just to satisfy your curiosity, Tiarnan? From what I recall there were two of us in the room that night, and there was a significant amount of time before you called a halt to proceedings. To be perfectly honest, I don't think I *do* want to give you the satisfaction of filling a void in your memory.'

And right at that moment Kate had felt as if she really *did* have the strength to walk away. The pain of his rejection was vivid all over again—right up until Tiarnan had hauled her into his chest, captured her close and kissed her, turning her world upside down and all her lofty intentions into dust. Desire had quickly burnt away any remaining paltry resistance.

He'd pulled back finally, when she'd been pliant and dazed in his arms, and said mockingly, 'What about giving *yourself* the satisfaction, Kate? Can you be honest enough with yourself to do that?'

Shockingly aware of his arousal, and knowing with an awful sense of futility that she didn't have the strength to walk away, she'd just said shakily, 'If we do this, Tiarnan, it's going to be on *my* terms. This affair ends when the holiday ends...'

'Katie? Are you there? Did you hear me?'

Kate came back from the memory of the bone-shattering intensity of that kiss. 'I heard you, Sorch. I know what I'm doing.'

She just hoped she sounded convincing.

'Katie, you know Tiarnan almost as well as me. He's always been adamant that he's not going to settle down again. And I just don't want—'

'Sorcha.' Kate cut her off before she could go any further. 'Look, I know what to expect. I'm going into this with my eyes wide open. Please just trust me. It's something we both need to...get closure on.' She winced at how trite that sounded, even though they were exactly the words she'd used to rationalise all this to herself only hours before.

Kate heard a baby's mewl in the background.

'You'd better go, Sorch. Molly sounds like she's waking up.'

Sorcha finally got off the phone, grumbling about the fact that she should have noticed that there'd been more to the tension between Kate and Tiarnan over the years than mutual antipathy.

Kate sat looking into space for a long moment. She knew that she couldn't turn away from this now. She knew that this was the only likely way to even *begin* getting over Tiarnan properly. But she was very afraid that Sorcha was right: that as distant as she planned to keep herself from emotional involvement with Tiarnan, she was already fighting a losing battle...

CHAPTER FIVE

THE following day Kate followed Tiarnan across the tarmac of the airport in Madrid to his private jet. He was hand-in-hand with a still serious-looking Rosie. As he'd said, Rosie had welcomed the news that Kate was coming with them—much to Kate's relief—but she still couldn't quite figure out the tension between father and daughter. Tiarnan looked back at her in that moment, making Kate's breath catch in her throat. He was wearing jeans and a plain polo shirt which made him look astoundingly gorgeous.

'We're flying to New York. I'm leaving my plane there and we'll be taking a smaller plane down to Martinique.'

Kate just nodded and forced a smile. What she also knew was that, far from just leaving his plane in New York, he was leaving it to be used by the philanthropic organisation he'd set up, which covered a multitude of charities he chaired or had set up. It was a very public move he'd made some years ago, to try and discourage the unnecessary use of private aircraft. Kate also knew he took commercial flights wherever possible.

She cursed him under her breath, her eyes drawn with dismaying inevitability to the perfection of his tautly muscled behind in the snug and faded jeans. The man was practically a saint, which made it so much harder to keep herself distanced. But from now on that was what she had to be—distanced. She was a woman of the world, sophisticated and experienced. Not shy, gauche Kate who quivered inwardly at the thought of what lay ahead.

Once they were settled onto the plane and it had taken off, Kate was relieved to see Tiarnan take out some paperwork. She and Rosie set up a card game at the other end of the plane. They were served a delicious lunch, after which Kate and Rosie had exhausted all the card games they knew—so Rosie started reading and Kate went back to her seat to try and get some sleep.

Tiarnan glanced over at her and Kate noticed that he looked tired. Her heart clenched, and she had the bizarre desire to go over and sweep away all his paperwork and force him to relax. Her cheeks warmed guiltily when she thought of how she'd like to make him relax. Already that precious distance was disappearing into the dust.

His head gestured towards the back of the plane, a glint in his eye. 'You can lie down in the bedroom if you want.'

Kate shook her head and tried to stem the heat rising in her body, which had reacted to that explicit glint. 'No, it's fine. Rosie's in there reading; she'll probably fall asleep.'

He just looked at her. After a moment he shrugged minutely and went back to his work. Kate reclined her chair and curled up, facing the other way.

Eventually the tension left her body. She was relieved that since that kiss in his study he'd been the personification of cool, polite distance. For all the world as if she were nothing more than a family friend joining them for a holiday. She would have been scared off if he'd been any other way: triumphant or gloating. But Kate didn't doubt that Tiarnan was a master in the handling of women, and even though that realisation hit her in the solar plexus she was too exhausted after a couple of sleepless nights to feel enraged.

When Kate's body had stopped moving, and it was obvious she was asleep, Tiarnan put down his paperwork and looked over. A tight coil of tension seemed to start in his feet and go all the way to his head. He allowed his eyes to rove over her form, taking in the deliciously round provocation of her bottom as it stuck out, straight at him, encased in linen trousers through which he could see the faint outline of her pants. Her legs were curled up, shoes off. Golden hair billowed out across the cushion and her head was tucked down into her chest. He got up silently and took down a blanket from overhead, spread it out over her body. In profile her face was relaxed, with none of that wakeful watchfulness that she seemed to subject him to, her big blue eyes wary.

He'd had to fight to control himself since he'd kissed her in his study. He'd expected to feel a certain level of disappointment in her acquiescence, which was such a contradiction when all he'd wanted was for her to say yes. And yet she hadn't been coquettish, she hadn't been calculating. When she'd stood in front of him in his study, strangely defiant, she'd had faint bruises of colour under her eyes, and if anything he might have guessed that she'd spent a sleepless night.

He stood straight and looked down at her. A surge of possessiveness gripped him. None of that mattered now. What mattered was that she was here, and very soon he would be discovering all the secrets of that luscious body. He turned abruptly before he did something stupid, like kiss her while she slept, and went to check on Rosie.

Kate woke to the sound of heated voices. Rosie and Tiarnan. She sat up and felt thoroughly dishevelled. She pushed her hair back from her face as she heard Tiarnan's voice emerge from the bedroom at the back.

'Rosalie Quinn, I will not continue this discussion until you can talk to me in a civil manner.'

Kate looked around, and her eyes widened as she saw Tiarnan standing in the doorway with hands on hips, obviously facing Rosie. And then she heard a tearful, 'Go *away!* I hate you, Tiarnan. Why should I listen to you when you're not even my real dad?'

And then a paroxysm of crying started. The door slammed in Tiarnan's face. He sighed deeply and jiggled the knob.

'Rosie, come on…'

Then, as if he could feel her eyes on him, he looked around and saw Kate. He ran a hand through his hair and walked up the cabin towards her, dwarfing everything around him as he did so.

'I'm sorry—we woke you.'

Kate just shook her head. 'It's fine…is everything OK?' Patently it wasn't.

Tiarnan sat in his seat, tipped his had back for a moment. 'Not really, no.'

He looked at her then, and Kate felt speared by the intensity of his eyes and the pain she could see in the blue depths.

'I should be honest with you, Kate. Rosie—well, it's a little more complicated than just moving schools—'

Just then the captain's voice interrupted, to announce that they were approaching New York and to get ready for landing. Kate had no idea she'd slept that long.

After the steward had come to make sure they were all awake, Kate said softly, 'Do you want me to go and—?'

Tiarnan shook his head. 'No, I'll get her. It's not your problem, Kate, and I'm sorry you had to hear anything. I'll explain later.'

After a few minutes a white-faced and obviously upset Rosie came out with Tiarnan and strapped herself into her seat.

As they landed and went through the formalities to change planes, Kate did her best to be upbeat and chirpy, to try and take Rosie's mind off whatever tension was between her and her father. She'd said that Tiarnan wasn't her real dad. Kate had no clue what that could be about. Sorcha had never mentioned anything.

By the time they'd boarded a smaller yet equally luxurious plane for Martinique, Rosie was obviously wrung out, and after picking at a meal she let Kate put her to bed in a small cabin in the back. Kate stayed with her till she fell asleep, feeling a very inappropriate level of maternal concern.

When she emerged to take her seat again Tiarnan asked, 'Do you want a drink?'

Kate shook her head, and then changed her mind abruptly, 'Actually, a small Baileys might be nice.'

Within seconds it was being offered to her by the steward on a tray. Once they were alone again, she could feel Tiarnan looking at her.

She turned to face him, and finally he said, 'I've decided to go to Martinique now with Rosie not only because of the school closing but also because we both need a break, and our house there is her favourite place in the world. It always has been. It's where she gets all the maternal love and affection I can't give her.'

Or her mother, evidently, Kate thought to herself. But she said nothing. Tiarnan was looking into his glass, swirling the liquid. Outside the window beside him the sky was a clear blue, strewn with white ribbons of clouds.

He looked at her and smiled a small smile. 'Mama Lucille and Papa Joe are like grandparents to Rosie. They've been the caretakers of my house since before I owned it, and they have five children and dozens of grandkids—all around Rosie's age. When we go there Rosie can disappear for days and I know she's fine. She turns into something almost feral with all her adopted family... I'm hoping that perhaps—'

He stopped, and the word *adopted* struck her. Kate asked quietly, 'What did she mean about you not being her real dad?'

He looked at her, and something intensely bleak crossed his face for a second before it was gone, making Kate think she'd imagined it.

'I'm not.'

Kate shook her head, frowning. 'But you are. I mean—'

He shook his head and downed his drink. His jaw clenched.

'No, I'm not. I believed I was until a couple of years ago. And I'd probably have never found out if Rosie hadn't got ill and had to have some blood tests done.'

He glanced at Kate. 'It was nothing serious, but we found out that her blood type didn't match mine. That isn't unusual in itself, but other tests were done and, to cut a long story short, I found out that Rosie is not my biological daughter.'

Kate just shook her head, frowning. 'But if you're not, then—'

'Who is?' He laughed sharply. 'Take your pick. It could be any one of the three or four men that Stella slept with around the time we split up.'

'Oh, Tiarnan, I'm sorry.'

His mouth was a grim line. 'The others weren't as wealthy or well set-up as me, so when Stella found out she was pregnant she decided to make me the father. A gamble that paid off. She had all the evidence, doctor's notes, and the dates seemed to match up. And I, who'd never wanted to find myself in that predicament, suddenly discovered a hitherto unknown paternal instinct, a sense of moral responsibility to do the right thing, so I proposed to Stella.'

Kate felt as if a stake were being driven into her heart. She tried to keep her face as bland as possible, not to allow that pain to surface—the pain she'd felt as a vulnerable eighteen-year-old who'd dreamed for a second that perhaps Tiarnan Quinn might fall for her in the space of one kiss.

'Stella married me and milked that paternal instinct for all it was worth. And then as soon as Rosie was born she was off—back to her current lover. We divorced soon after, she got a nice settlement—and the rest, as they say, is history.'

Kate knew that was an understatement. Stella Rios had made a small fortune out of Tiarnan. It had been all over the news at the time. Her head pounded with questions: Had he loved her, though, despite that reluctance to settle down? Was that why he'd married her, apart from wanting to do the right thing? Had she broken his heart?

Kate's throat felt dry. 'When did you find out about the other men?'

Tiarnan closed his eyes for a moment and rubbed a hand over his face. 'When I confronted Stella with the fact that Rosie wasn't mine.' He looked at Kate again. 'I officially adopted Rosie as soon as I discovered the truth. Luckily Stella had signed complete custody over to me on our divorce. There was no way I was going to allow her any opportunity to use Rosie as some kind of pawn in an effort to get more money. Which was exactly what she did as soon as she realised that I knew. But thankfully by then Rosie was mine, and Stella knows well that taking on a small child would disrupt her hedonistic life-style, so she's never contested.'

Kate could see that, despite finding out Rosie wasn't his daughter, in every sense she obviously meant as much to him, if not more, than if she *had* been biologically his. It made her feel an ache inside. This wasn't the Tiarnan she was used to— calculating and ruthless and a little intimidating. This Tiarnan was far more human.

'I only allow Rosie to see Stella because she wishes it. Invariably she returns upset every time, but no matter what happens she always wants to go back.' Tiarnan shook his head incredulously, clearly not understanding the apparently mas-ochistic instinct of his ten-year-old daughter. 'Over a year ago I went to Buenos Aires to pick Rosie up from a visit. She over-heard Stella and I arguing...she heard every word...unfortu-nately it was all about the adoption. At first Rosie refused to come home with me, but when Stella told her in no uncertain terms that she wasn't welcome to stay with her any longer, she had no choice...'

Horror coursed through Kate that a mother could be so cruel. She put a hand to her mouth. 'Oh that poor, poor child.'

Tiarnan looked grim. 'And yet Rosie still goes back. Still wants to see Stella even though she's been so unutterably cruel.'

Kate shook her head. She could feel Rosie's pain acutely. In some ways it was similar to what she'd endured with her own mother for years.

Tiarnan looked bleak again. 'I haven't even told Sorcha yet because I don't want to rake up her own painful memories.'

Kate knew what Tiarnan was referring to. When Sorcha and Tiarnan's father had died, Sorcha had found out that she'd actually been born to the mistress of her father—his secretary. She'd died in childbirth, and Tiarnan's Spanish mother had taken Sorcha in as her own. But they'd never really got on, and finding out the truth had sent Sorcha into dark turmoil which could have resulted in a tragedy but thankfully hadn't. Unfortunately Sorcha and Tiarnan's mother had had an even more estranged relationship ever since.

Tiarnan's voice cut through Kate's memories. 'Rosie is punishing me for this…'

Kate looked at him and answered instinctively. 'Because she can. She knows deep down that you love her, so she's lashing out at you when she really wants to lash out at her mother, for rejecting her. She just wants her mother to love her…that's all.'

Tiarnan's mouth thinned. 'I hope you're right. I could cope with anything if I knew that for sure. It's been a tough year.'

Looking into Kate's eyes, Tiarnan had a sudden sense of being out of control. He'd only ever revealed the truth of his marriage to one or two people, and that had been out of pure necessity. His own sister didn't even know about Rosie. And yet here he was, blithely spilling his secrets to a woman whose presence in his life was solely down to the desire he felt for her.

As if to drive away his disturbing thoughts, and an unwelcome feeling of vulnerability, he reached over and with effortless strength pulled Kate from her seat.

She landed on his lap, off balance, her hands against his

chest. Breathless, she said, 'Tiarnan, stop—we can't…not here. What if Rosie—?'

'Rosie could sleep through a bomb going off.' He quirked a sad smile. 'I used to think that she got that from me…'

An unbidden wave of tenderness and compassion came over Kate, taking her by surprise. 'Well maybe she did in another way. Biological ties can be highly overrated, you know.'

A dark brow arched. 'You sound like you speak from experience. Anything you'd like to share? What skeletons are in *your* closet, Kate?'

She shook her head and ignored the dart of pain that struck her. Her skeletons were dull and boring. She thought of her stressed-out, harassed father and her vacuous, narcissistic mother. Kate hadn't seen her flighty mother, currently on rich husband number four, for nearly a year—and that wasn't unusual. She didn't want to allow that old familiar pain to rise now. It would make her think of her yearning to create a solid, loving family base. She couldn't think of that here and now, feeling so raw after what Tiarnan had just shared.

Kate became very aware of being cradled in Tiarnan's lap. And very aware of a shockingly hard piece of his anatomy. When he tugged on her hair to pull her face closer she was powerless to resist. She felt as if a layer of skin had been stripped away, leaving her even more vulnerable to him. She touched her open mouth to his, breaths intermingling and weaving together. Their tongue-tips met, retreated. Breathing and heart-rates increased. Kate could feel his other hand drag her body even closer, and in an instant the kiss had changed from tentative and exploratory to full-on passion, mouths fused, tongues dancing an erotic dance.

After long, heady seconds Kate could feel the whirlpool of pleasure threatening to suck her down. Tiarnan pulled back, his chest still hard against hers. She made a sound of frustration when he broke away. She felt flushed, dizzy, breathless.

Smoky blue eyes glittered up into hers. 'You're probably right. Now is not the time…'

Sanity returned, and Kate pushed herself away from his chest with trembling hands. 'No, it's not.'

She stood up unsteadily and wobbled back to her own seat, snapping her belt shut across her lap, as if it might afford her some protection from the man she would have allowed to make love to her sitting right there in the seat if not for the fact that he'd stopped. In that moment she knew she had to protect herself—had to make Tiarnan see that this affair was on *her* terms and had limits.

She took a deep breath and looked at him, forcing herself not to notice the way his flushed cheeks, tousled hair, the almost feral glitter in his eyes that connected to something deep inside her with visceral intensity.

'Tiarnan, look—'

'That sounds ominous.'

Kate cursed him. 'We need to talk about…*this*.' She cast a quick look back to the closed cabin door, even though there was no way anyone could hear their softly spoken words. 'This has to end when we return home.'

His eyes flashed. Kate knew he probably wasn't used to his lovers dictating terms. Well, tough. This was the only way she knew would be able to get through this. This would be her great indulgence. She knew better than anybody after those revelations that Tiarnan was not the marrying or settling down kind. Once these ten days were over she would be getting on with the rest of her life. No matter how hard. She had to. She couldn't contemplate another moment of this lingering pain.

She forged on. 'I mean it, Tiarnan. I don't want to add to Rosie's woes by causing her more turmoil.'

Tiarnan's whole body bristled at that. 'Neither do I, Kate. I wouldn't have asked you here in a heartbeat if I thought it might result in upsetting Rosie. She wants you here too, and she won't see anything to upset her. If she'd expressed the slightest doubt about you coming I wouldn't have asked you.'

Kate immediately felt chagrined. 'Of course not. I know you wouldn't do anything— But I'd just be afraid of her seeing…something.' How could she not, Kate wailed inwardly, when all she had to do was look at Tiarnan and feel herself going up in flames…

Tiarnan finally looked away, after a long, intense moment, and seemed to spot something out of Kate's window. He came out of his seat to lean over her. Kate squirmed backwards, terrified he'd feel the peaking of her nipples against his arm, the evidence of how easily he could turn her on.

He pointed at something. 'Look—there it is.'

Kate looked down and, sure enough, an idyllic-looking island of forested green rose out of the unbelievably azure water around it. Mountain-tops and peaks were visible through the clouds.

Just then the cabin door opened, and Kate felt Tiarnan tense. Acting on pure instinct, she took his hand for a moment and squeezed it before he stood up to greet Rosie. He flashed her an enigmatic look. Immediately she felt silly, exposed. Who did she think she was? His wife?

'I was just showing Kate Martinique. We'll be landing soon.'

Tiarnan was barely aware of Rosie ignoring him as she came and sat on Kate's lap, pointing things out to her through the window. He sat down and could still feel the press of Kate's fingers around his. A show of support. He'd never had that— never had that sensation of someone sharing his experience. It made him feel— He didn't want to think about how it made him feel. Or how it felt to see Rosie sitting on Kate's lap with such trusting ease, their two heads close together.

Kate's assertion that she wouldn't want Rosie to be hurt had made all sorts of hackles rise. *He* was the one responsible for his daughter's well-being and security, and he had the uncustomary sensation of having allowed himself and her to be put in a vulnerable position. With an effort, he let himself tune into Rosie's chatter to Kate about Mama Lucille and Papa Joe, and her best friend Zoe.

Still feeling exposed, and studiously avoiding looking anywhere near Tiarnan, Kate hugged Rosie's skinny frame close until she had to take her own seat. Kate hated that her heart ached so much for Rosie and Tiarnan's distress. She shouldn't be allowing them to get too close. But as the plane touched down in a bright tropical paradise, all she could feel was a bittersweet joy so intense that she had to shield her face with her hair, terrified that Tiarnan or Rosie might see it.

With the time difference, it was afternoon when they arrived. The sun beat down, and it must have rained shortly before as the ground was steaming. The air was heavy and humid, warming right through to Kate's bones and already making sweat gather at the small of her back and between her breasts.

A smiling young local man met them off the plane, with a small open-top Jeep, and Tiarnan drove it now on a narrow road along the coast. They were heading south, and Kate was happy just to take in the scenery and listen to Rosie chatting non-stop about everything and anything. It was good to see her so animated.

Before too long they came into a charming fishing village, Anse D'Arlet with a white church dominating the seafront and a long wooden promenade that stretched out over the water, where colourful boats bobbed up and down. Shops were strewn along the main street. Some of the buildings were crumbling and had a faded grandeur that just added to the appeal of this slow, peaceful-looking place.

'This is it—our local village.'

Kate looked at Tiarnan briefly. Even he already looked more relaxed.

Rosie was standing up behind his seat, pointing a finger, and she said excitedly, 'That's Zoe's house—there, Katie, look! Tiarnan, please can I get out and go see her now?'

Kate could see Tiarnan's jaw clench, and she felt his pain at Rosie's insistent use of *Tiarnan*. He looked for a moment as if he was going to say no, but then he slowed the Jeep at the bottom of a small drive and Rosie jumped out. Another small girl appeared, and the two started squealing and running towards each other. Tiarnan waved at the woman who had appeared in the doorway of the house, and Kate guessed it must be the little girl's mother.

He turned then and shook his head at Kate. 'See? We'll be lucky to get her back for dinner, but she'll want to see Mama Lucille…'

Tiarnan kept driving southwards out of the small town, and after a couple of minutes turned right towards the sea into an open set of gates that were wildly overgrown with frangipani and exotic flowers. They emerged from under a dense canopy of foliage into a small forecourt in front of an idyllic white-painted villa.

It was old colonial French-style, and had a wooden deck wrapped around it and what looked like a long balcony above, with an intricately carved railing. Shutters were painted bright blue, and everything looked pristine and lovingly cared for. A shape appeared in the open front door, and Kate saw a huge, buxom woman with the biggest, whitest smile she'd ever seen in her life.

Tiarnan had stopped the Jeep, and as he helped her out he smiled and said, 'May I present the inimitable Mama Lucille…?'

The woman came to the top of the steps and put her hands on ample hips. She looked from left to right. 'Where is my baby girl?'

Tiarnan took the steps two at a time and gave her a huge hug before standing back, 'Where do you think? She had to stop and see her partner in crime—*your* granddaughter Zoe. No doubt they're already driving Anne-Marie crazy.'

Mama Lucille shook her head and laughed a big belly laugh,

and as Kate came shyly up the steps behind Tiarnan she could see that this woman truly was some sort of universal earth mother. She looked ageless.

Mama Lucille set Tiarnan aside and put her hands on her hips again. 'And who is *this* vision?' She glanced at Tiarnan with a wicked gleam in her dark eyes. 'Is she an angel come to save us all?'

Before Tiarnan could answer, Kate stepped forward and smiled. 'No angel, I'm afraid—just Kate. I'm an old friend of Tiarnan and Sorcha's.'

Kate's innate humility struck Tiarnan forcibly. She was one of the most famous models in the world, but she had absolutely no evidence of an ego to reflect that; no expectation that people should *know* her. The realisation unsettled him for a moment, and he had to concede that Kate was surprising him—exactly as she'd done in San Francisco, when he'd imagined things going differently. He was somewhat belatedly aware that he didn't really know her that well at all, and with that awareness came a tingling sense of anticipation.

Kate was holding out her hand, but Mama Lucille waved it away and dragged Kate into her massive bosom. 'Any friend of theirs is a friend of mine.' She pulled back then and held Kate away from her slightly, looked her up and down critically. 'Are you a model, the same as that sister of his?'

Kate nodded.

'Hmph. Thought so. Too skinny—just like that other one—but I'd say she's bigger now, after the baby!' Mama Lucille guffawed again and pinched Kate's cheek. 'Don't you worry, angel. A few days of my cooking and we'll put some fat on those hips…'

Kate had to laugh as she imagined her agent's horrorstruck face if she arrived back a few pounds heavier, and with that came the familiar yearning to just let go and stop being so aware of things like her weight.

Before she knew it, Mama Lucille had disappeared in a flurry of movement, with a promise of some dinner in a couple of hours. A young girl with a shy pretty smile appeared and took their bags into the house.

Tiarnan took Kate by the hand. She would have pulled away, but he held her with easy strength, looking at her with an assessing gaze that made her toes curl.

'Come on, I'll give you the tour.'

Kate felt dizzy by the time Tiarnan was leading her upstairs. The house was completely charming. All dark polished wooden floorboards, white walls and beautiful old furniture. White muslin curtains fluttered in the breezes that flowed through open sash windows, with latticed shutters wide open. She'd seen a butterfly dart in one window and out through the next with a flash of bright iridescence. It was truly a home. Kate could imagine the doors always open, people coming and going all day, and yet it had a tranquil air that beguiled and seduced…

'Do Mama Lucille and Papa Joe live here too?' Kate asked as she followed Tiarnan up the stairs and tried not to look at his bottom. He glanced back and she coloured guiltily.

'No. Even though I've been trying to get them to move in for years. They're on the other side of the property. There's a back entrance, down by the private beach, and they live in the old gate lodge. Mama Lucille says she prefers it because there's not enough room for her family to come and stay, and it's the only way she and Papa Joe get peace and quiet to themselves.'

Clearly, from the warmth in his voice, Tiarnan was as crazy as Rosie was about this place and the people. It made Kate's heart do a funny jump in her chest. And what also made her heart feel funny was that the same impression she'd had on the plane: she'd never seen this more relaxed side of Tiarnan before. There'd always been something slightly aloof about him, distant and distinguished. Formidable. And here all that was being stripped away. *Distance—keep your distance,* she repeated like a mantra in her head, futile as she knew it was.

She got to the top of the stairs to see a wide open corridor, doorways on each side, and a huge window seat at the end with what she could imagine must be a spectacular view over the garden. Tiarnan was leaning nonchalantly against a door that led into a bedroom.

'This is your room.'

Kate looked at him warily as she passed him and went in. Her bag had already been deposited inside. The same lovingly polished floorboards were echoed in the antique furniture. Old black and white photographs hung on the walls. A huge four-poster bed was in the centre of the room, its muslin drapes pulled back. A small door led to a white-tiled bathroom with a huge stand-alone bath and shower in the corner. It screamed understated luxury. A pair of open veranda doors led out to the second level wooden balcony, along which trailed vine-like flowers of colours so vibrant it almost hurt to look at them. And beyond that lay the unmistakable clear blue waters of the Caribbean. This truly *was* paradise.

She turned at the open door and looked back at Tiarnan, her heart thumping heavily. 'It's beautiful. Really.'

He walked towards her with all the grace and danger of a dark panther, and Kate could feel her eyes grow bigger as he came closer. Her loose linen trousers and shirt suddenly felt constricting, but he just took her hand and led her outside and to the left, where she could see an identical set of open doors. He stopped at the entrance and Kate could see another room, a little bigger and obviously decorated along much more masculine lines. *His room.*

He didn't even have to say it. The understanding was heavy between them. Within this stunning house and these two rooms they were as effectively cut off and private as they wanted to be. He let go of her hand and looked down at her. Kate felt unbearably hot right then, and it had nothing to do with being in the tropics.

He gestured with his head back to her room. 'That used to be Rosie's room when she was smaller, so I could hear if she woke during the night, but she hasn't slept there for a few years. Her room is on the other side of the villa. This balcony isn't accessible except by these two rooms.' He took her hand and raised it to his mouth, kissing it briefly, his eyes searing down into hers. 'All you have to do is let me know…'

Kate gulped. 'Tiarnan, I…' She stopped. She couldn't fight the inevitable—couldn't *not* own up to her own desire. So finally she just said weakly, 'OK.'

Sudden trepidation assailed her. He must be assuming that she'd had plenty of practice in the last ten years, and while she hadn't been celibate, she hadn't exactly been swinging from the rafters either. He certainly wouldn't be getting the sophisticated seduction he was no doubt used to and expecting!

He let her hand go and stepped back. 'Why don't you rest up and settle in? Mama Lucille will be serving dinner in a couple of hours…'

He stood there, silhouetted by the sun, looking taller and leaner and darker than she could ever remember him being, and Kate felt almost paralysed by the strength of her desire. When she finally could, she just nodded, and turned and fled.

CHAPTER SIX

THAT evening Kate looked blankly at her clothes laid out on the bed. Luckily she'd been able to go shopping in Madrid to pick up some more things. Tiarnan had offered to buy them for her, but her withering look at that suggestion had made him throw his hands up and step back saying, 'Fine—I've just never known a woman to turn down a chance of a free shopping trip.'

Kate's hackles had risen—and a sense of having made a monumental error. 'Well, I'm not every other woman out there, and I can afford to dress myself—thank you all the same.'

Her mind returned to the present, but with a lingering after-taste of the jealousy she'd felt when he'd alluded to dressing other women. She forced it from her mind. She was well aware that she was going to be the latest in a long line of Tiarnan Quinn's conquests. He was nothing if not discreet about his lovers, and Kate knew that was to protect Rosie—but, coming from the world she came from, she was well aware of the gossip that told of the countless beauties he'd bedded over the years, all of whom had been left with extravagantly generous gifts. Kate vowed there and then that she would not be the same. No trinket, no matter how expensive, would be lavished on her at the end of this. Even the thought of it made her burn with humiliation.

She finally focused on the clothes in front of her again. What did one wear to dinner with the man who'd stolen your heart for what felt like all your life? Kate felt the colour drain from her face and she pressed a hand to her chest, feeling suddenly constricted. He hadn't stolen her heart. *He hadn't*. How could he have? She'd had a teenage crush that had culminated in the single most shattering moment of her life. That was all. She hadn't spent enough time with him to fall in love with him. That night had ripped away any rose-tinted views she might have had of love. And she certainly hadn't come close since.

She couldn't love someone like Tiarnan. He was too hard, too forceful. Too obviously driven to succeed—like her father. She'd always pictured herself with someone kind, gentle…unassuming.

This was just going to be a brief interlude. A completion of something that *she* had started a long time ago. She was doing this so that she could move on with her life and banish Tiarnan Quinn from all the corners of her mind in which he still lingered. She wasn't in love with him, she was in lust. That was all.

The constriction in her chest eased, Kate breathed deep. And finally managed to choose something to wear.

When she came downstairs and approached the door leading out to the wooden terrace at the back of the house a short while later, she could hear Tiarnan's deep rumble of a voice and Mama Lucille's infectious belly laugh. Kate felt unaccountably self-conscious all over again, and resisted the urge to smooth sweaty palms on the dress she'd chosen. It was plain and simple, as only the best designer clothes could be. She'd picked out something that helped her to feel covered up—a deep royal blue silk maxi-dress. She knew how lucky she was that because of her profession she'd never lacked for beautiful clothes, and she was glad of the armour now—as if she could somehow project an image that Tiarnan would be familiar with: an elegant and nonchalant lover.

But when she took a deep breath and walked out Tiarnan looked up. His eyes locked onto hers, and she immediately felt undressed, despite the ankle-length dress, and regretted pulling her hair back into a low ponytail, wishing she had it loose, to cover her face. The silk seemed to cling and caress her body with indecent eagerness. All nonchalance fled and the churning turmoil was back with a vengeance as every step brought her closer and closer to that glittering blue gaze that swept up and down her body, leaving what felt like a trail of fire in its wake.

For a second, as Kate walked towards him, Tiarnan's brain went completely blank and every coherent thought was replaced with heat. She was a vision in blue silk that seemed to waft around her body and yet cling to every curve with a lover's touch. He looked down, and his chest tightened with an indefinable emotion when he saw that her feet were bare. The heat in his brain intensified, and only Mama Lucille pointedly clearing her throat stopped him from turning into a drooling speechless idiot. Some of the most beautiful women in the world had appeared similarly dressed before him, for his pleasure, yet they had never had this paralysing effect on him. He managed to stand just as Kate got to the table, her delicate scent reaching his nostrils as he pulled out her chair and she sat down with a warm smile directed at Mama Lucille.

Her colour was high and she was avoiding his eye, making Tiarnan feel unaccountably flustered. He ignored Mama Lucille's explicit look, which seemed to bore a hole in his head, and thankfully she bustled off with her young assistant in tow.

Kate struggled to get her heartbeat and her breathing under control. The dress which had felt so appropriate now felt like the most inappropriate thing she could have chosen. When she felt sufficiently calm she flicked a glance to Tiarnan. He was staring at her with hooded eyes. Against her volition, her eyes dropped, taking in the snowy-white shirt, open at the neck, and the dark trousers. His hair was damp, as if he'd showered not long ago, and Kate could feel heat climbing upwards over her chest. She grabbed her napkin and clung onto it, twisting it under the table.

'Where's Rosie?'

Tiarnan's eyes didn't move from hers. 'She came back here earlier with Zoe, for dinner with Mama Lucille. Zoe's mother, Anne-Marie, collected them just before you came down. She's spending the night at their place. It's something of a tradition. She'll be back in the morning.'

Kate looked down for a moment. *They were alone all night?* Her heart was thudding heavily, unevenly. Right then she wished for Rosie's comforting presence, even with the tension between father and daughter. 'She's having fun, then…'

Tiarnan nodded. 'Yes. She's surrounded by people who love her like their own, and it's important for her to have that while she's determined to reject me.'

Kate looked at him, unable not to, touched deeply by his concern that Rosie feel loved even while she was determined not to accept love from him. In her experience parents either ignored their children or resented them. And yet he was doing his utmost to make sure Rosie was secure.

'You're a good father, Tiarnan.' She cursed herself for sounding so husky and trite. And cursed herself again when she could feel that armour she'd put up around herself crumble ever so slightly. In an instant he had smashed aside her assertion that he was a man like her father—too career-orientated to care about his daughter.

To her relief Mama Lucille returned with a steaming bowl, followed by Eloise, the girl who'd helped with the luggage and who Mama Lucille now introduced as one of her older granddaughters. Kate got up instinctively to help, but Mama Lucille ordered her to, 'Sit! Let us serve you now.'

Kate watched as more plates arrived, with what looked like an impressive array of fish and roasted vegetables and rice and potatoes and salad. Her eyes were wide, watching as Tiarnan poured white wine into glasses so cold they still had mist on them.

'I've never seen so much food in my life.'

He took her plate and proceeded to heap it high with the succulent food, saying drily, 'Don't tell me you're one of these women who prefer to push a lettuce leaf around your plate and watch it wither and die rather than eat it?'

'No,' Kate said quickly, taking the plate he handed her. 'I couldn't think of anything worse. My problem has never been lack of appetite, it's stopping myself eating.' She grimaced for a second. 'Unfortunately, unlike your sister and presumably you too, I can't eat everything around me and stay the same size. All I eat has to come off again.'

Tiarnan fought down the urge to let his eyes rove over her curves. She was right. Where Sorcha was lean and athletic, Kate had a more natural voluptuousness, a sexy lushness. He picked up his glass and waited for Kate to do the same.

Kate was intensely aware of the way the dusk was claiming the setting sun, turning the sky smoky mauve. The breeze was warm and the sound of the sea came from nearby. Small flaming lights nearby lit up the table and surrounding area. It was idyllic.

Tiarnan held up his glass and said, 'I thought it would be nicer to eat out here. I hope it's not too rustic for you?'

Kate shook her head, mesmerised, and picked up her glass. 'It's perfect. I love it.'

He touched his glass to hers and it made the most subtle chime. 'Welcome, Kate, and *bon appetit.*'

'*Bon appetite,*' she mumbled, her face flaming, and she took a quick sip of the deliciously dry wine.

Tiarnan made sure she had everything she needed, and then proceeded to fill up his own plate impressively. Kate didn't doubt for a second that a man like him would have a huge appetite. When she thought of that, the heat which had begun to recede surged back. She groaned inwardly and then groaned out loud as she tasted a langoustine and it nearly melted on her tongue with an explosion of exquisite tastes.

'This,' she said, when she could. 'Is amazing.'

Tiarnan smiled and nodded. 'Mama Lucille's cooking is legendary. She's had countless offers to work for others, even from the best restaurants here on Martinique, but she's turned them all down.'

Kate smiled too, and picked up her wine glass. 'And no doubt you keep her very well…compensated?'

He inclined his head modestly. 'But of course. I look after everyone I love.'

Kate's heart clenched, and she speared some more food to distract him from what might be in her expression. Was he also talking about the way he compensated his lovers so well? Did he, on some level, love them all too? In that easy superficial way that some men did? Only to let them go easily when they got too clingy? Was he capable of truly falling in love?

'What about you, Kate? Would you like children some day? You're good with Rosie—you seem to have a natural affinity…'

She just about managed not to choke on her wine, and put down the glass carefully, a little blindsided by his swift change of subject. Normally, with such a question from someone else, her natural inclination to reply honestly that she'd never wanted anything more would make answering easy. But here, now, with Tiarnan, she had to protect herself.

She shrugged one shoulder and looked down. 'Yes, I've thought of it. What woman my age doesn't?' Her voice was light, unconcerned, but her womb seemed to contract as she battled a sudden vivid image of holding a dark-haired baby in her arms, Tiarnan's head coming close to press a kiss against the downy, sweet-smelling skin.

In complete dismay at her wayward imagination, and in rejection of that image, she looked up almost defiantly, feeling brittle. 'But not yet. I'm not ready to be tied down. I'm sure it'll happen some day, though, when I meet the right person.'

Tiarnan lounged back. Kate could imagine his long legs

stretched out easily under the table. In comparison she felt incredibly uptight and tense.

'And you haven't met the right person yet, I take it?'

'Well, I'd hardly be here now if I had, would I?' She cursed herself for letting him get to her, making her sound snappy. Tiarnan's eyes had become assessing. Looking deep.

He shrugged too. 'I wouldn't know, Kate. To be honest, it wouldn't surprise me in the least. Let's just say that in my experience women are perennially unsatisfied—either with themselves or their lives—and will do whatever it takes to relieve their boredom.'

'That's a very cynical view to have.'

He shrugged and took a sip of wine. 'When the first relationship you witness has deep flaws, it tends to colour everything else.'

Kate's prickliness dissolved in an instant. 'I know your parents didn't…get on.'

Tiarnan's mouth tightened. 'To put it mildly. I don't have to tell you what it was like… But if none of that had happened I wouldn't have Sorcha for a sister.'

Kate said quietly, 'The fact that your mother took Sorcha in as her own was pretty selfless.'

He made a rejecting motion with his hand. 'A selfless act which drove the wedge between her and my father, and ultimately Sorcha too, even deeper. My mother was—still is—a devout Catholic. She took Sorcha in more out of a sense of religious duty than anything else.'

They both fell silent for a moment, very aware of how that had caused such pain and hurt to Sorcha when she had found out. Kate knew instinctively that there was very little likelihood that Tiarnan would discuss this with anyone else—it was just because of who she was, and the fact that she knew already. Any intimacy she was feeling now was false.

Something rose up within Kate, compelling her to say quietly, 'I do believe, though, that it's possible.'

'That what's possible?'

'For people to be happy. I mean, look at Sorcha and Romain; they're happy.'

Tiarnan's face looked unbearably harsh in the flickering light of the candles for a moment. 'Yes, they are.' He sounded almost surprised, and then his voice became hard. 'I, however, learnt my lesson a long time ago. I indulged in the dream for a brief moment and saw the ugliest part of women's machinations, and how far they're prepared to go to feather their nest.'

Kate's heart clenched. He was talking about Stella, of course—and every other woman too, it would appear, by proxy.

Tiarnan looked into his wine glass, tension gripping him. He cursed himself again for allowing this woman to loosen his tongue, and forced down the tension. He looked up and caught Kate's eye, allowed himself to dive into the deep blue depths. He saw her exactly as she was: a woman of the world, successful, confident, single. Not afraid to take what she wanted. She was like him. Immediately he felt on a more even keel. He snaked out a hand and caught hers, revelling in the contact, the way her skin felt so warm and firm and silky. Revelling in the sensual anticipation.

'For people like us, however, things are different... We won't be caught like that, seduced by some empty dream.'

Kate's heart clenched so hard at that she had to hold in a gasp. She stung inside that he believed her to be the same as him. Ironically enough, out of his sister and Kate, Sorcha had been the more cynical of the two, constantly teasing Kate for her innate romantic streak, for her maternal instinct. Sorcha had been the one with the high walls of defence erected around her, and Romain had been the only man capable of gaining her trust, opening her heart...

Yet, despite her own largely loveless upbringing, Kate had somehow emerged clinging onto those maternal instincts and that romantic dream. And a very secret part of her was still doggedly clinging onto it, despite witnessing the cynicism of the man to whom she was willingly, *stupidly* planning to give herself, in the hope that perhaps it would cure her of this obsession. The fact that he believed her to be as jaded as he was surely had to be in her favour? Protection for when she would walk away? He would believe her to be in one piece, unmoved, moving on with blithe disregard to her next lover. And she would be, she told herself fiercely now. She'd be blithe if it killed her.

She wanted to ask him about his wife—ask if *she'd* managed to break through his cynical wall to make him believe in love for a brief moment. But even if she had, considering how she had deceived him about Rosie, it could only have reaffirmed his beliefs, made them even more entrenched.

Kate forced down all her questions and leaned forward to start eating again, even though her appetite seemed to have vanished. She smiled brilliantly.

'Well, then, we can rest easy in the protection such beliefs can offer us: no expectation, no disappointment.'

The words seemed to score through her heart like a serrated knife, they so went against her own personal philosophy. A philosophy she couldn't share with Tiarnan.

Tiarnan smiled lazily, eyes narrowed on hers. 'A kindred spirit. I couldn't have put it better.'

As Kate forced herself to eat and sip the wine, engage in conversation that moved away from darker topics, she told herself that at least now she was under no illusion that some kind of fairytale would happen here. Tiarnan was utterly content with his life and there was no way he was going to let in Kate to shake things up.

The plates were gone, Mama Lucille had bade them goodnight, and Kate had kissed her in thanks for the meal, making the older woman look embarrassed but happy. Papa Joe, her handsome husband, had come to collect her to walk her home. Being bowed with age didn't diminish his charm. He seemed as naturally friendly and happy as his wife, and they heard them laughing and conversing loudly in local French patois all the way down the garden path. Witnessing their happiness made Kate's conversation with Tiarnan over dinner feel all the more unbearably poignant.

The heavy perfumed air was alive with the sounds of insects. Kate felt almost painfully sensitive to everything. All too aware of what she yearned for and what she was prepared to settle for with Tiarnan. He reached out and took her hand, and predictably she tensed.

'You don't seem very relaxed.' He stated the obvious.

Kate shrugged and forced down her tangled thoughts of yearning. 'Despite what you might believe, I'm not used to being whisked halfway across the world to become a rich man's mistress for a few days.'

Tiarnan's jaw clenched. She kept talking about the time limit. And she certainly wasn't just a rich man's mistress. She was going to be *his* lover. Her words over dinner, her reassurance that she was like him, should be making him feel at ease, confident, and yet they weren't. Not entirely. He didn't trust her. And he didn't know why that rankled. What woman *did* he trust? He was used to not trusting women.

He drove away the questions. He had no need to question anything. Kate Lancaster was here, his for now, and that was all that mattered. They were wasting time. He studied her downbent head, the gleaming blonde hair, the satin smooth skin of her bared shoulders under the straps of her dress, the swell of her breasts…and he knew just how to drive away those thoughts, the tenseness which made ambiguous feelings run through him.

Tiarnan kept a hold of her hand and stood, tugging her up with him. Kate's eyes met his and the world seemed to stop turning momentarily. 'I know just what we need.'

'You do?'

Kate's voice came out like a squeak. She cursed her inability to sound insouciant when she needed to. He nodded, and started to walk back into the house, taking her with him, his grip strong and sure. Her legs felt like jelly. Panic started to rise up, strangling her. She had to tell him, had to say something. He thought she was something she wasn't...

'Tiarnan, I—'

He turned and pressed a finger to her lips.

'I'm taking you out.'

Confusion cut through the panic. The scarily vivid images of their naked limbs entwined on his bed faded.

'What? Where?'

He looked at her for a long moment, and then just said, 'Dancing.'

Kate's hand was still in Tiarnan's as he led them into a dimly lit bar not too far from the house. A throbbing pulsing beat of music enveloped them instantly, along with the heat of bodies and muted conversations.

He'd waited till she had put on some shoes and had obviously made a call, as an open-top Jeep with a smiling driver had been waiting for them outside the villa. He led her to the bar now, only letting go of her hand to put an arm around her waist and draw her in close. Kate saw the bartender spot him and come over with a huge smile on his face.

'Tiarnan, my man! It's good to see you.' The barman's openly curious and very flirty glance took Kate in with blatant appreciation.

She felt embarrassed, and very out of her depth. Tiarnan kept surprising her at every turn, and the thought that he might have read her trepidation and done this to somehow make things easier for her made her feel vulnerable.

'And your beautiful guest...'

For the first time in his life Tiarnan felt the intense spiking of jealousy as his old friend Luc looked Kate up and down with what seemed to be insulting impunity. He'd noticed every other man's head swivelling too, as they'd walked into the bar. Kate stood out like a magnificent bird of paradise.

Resisting the unfathomable urge to walk straight back out again, he forced himself to sound civil and say, 'Luc, good to see you too. We'll have two of your best rums.'

He looked down at Kate and was surprised to see her looking almost…self-conscious. He tugged her in closer and she looked up, a flare of colour racing across her cheekbones.

'Is that OK?'

Kate felt almost disembodied, looking up into Tiarnan's eyes. 'Is what OK?'

'Martinique rum—you should try it.'

She just nodded, still barely aware of what he was saying. Their solicitous host insisted on showing them over to a secluded booth with a view over the faded grandeur of the bar, which was open to the street, and the dark inkiness of the sea in the distance. They were in the ground floor of an old colonial building. The crowd were local, the music was a kind of sexy upbeat Salsa. And then it changed smoothly to something slow and *very* hot. Some of the couples on the dance floor certainly looked as if they were just moments away from disappearing to a dark corner where—

Kate willed down the intense blush she could feel on her face as she looked at the couples, and just then Tiarnan's hand cupped her jaw, turning her to face him. She felt feverish.

He shook his head, and a thumb moved back and forth across her cheek. 'Enchanting. I don't think I've ever seen anyone blush the way you do.'

Kate burned inside and out. The enormity of where she was and who she was sitting with was hitting her anew all over again. 'It's just my colouring.'

Their eyes stayed locked for a long moment, until Kate felt as if she was melting inside. Just as she was about to beg to be released from that intense gaze, Tiarnan suddenly broke it and looked away, making Kate feel absurdly bereft all of a sudden. She was a mass of contradictions and warring desires.

Tiarnan's friend approached with two glasses, and left again with a mischievous smile and a look that Kate didn't miss. When Tiarnan had introduced them briefly she'd thought he'd been uncharacteristically curt to the other man, but Luc didn't seem to mind. She took a sip of the dark liquid and coughed immediately, her eyes smarting.

Tiarnan quirked a brow and smiled. 'Strong stuff.'

Kate grabbed for some water and drank it down. 'You could have warned me.' She watched as Tiarnan took another sip himself, watched the way the strong column of his throat worked. At that moment the music changed back to an infectiously upbeat rhythm.

Tiarnan extended a hand across the table. 'Come on, let's dance.'

Kate shrank back with genuine fear. She could see couples dancing with effortless grace and style, making moves she could never even hope to mimic. She shook her head desperately, 'I can't dance, Tiarnan.'

He left his hand where it was.

'Seriously,' she said pleadingly. 'I'm really, really bad, I'll just embarrass you.'

He stood up and took her hand from her lap, pulling her up.

She tried to resist. 'I'll watch you dance with someone else—honestly.'

He wasn't listening. He pulled her remorselessly after him. Kate was having flashbacks to excruciating moments on other dance floors where she'd shuffled around, invariably much to Sorcha's hysterical amusement. Or memories of standing on various hapless men's feet and apologising profusely.

She tried to pull away again. 'Tiarnan, you don't understand. I've two left feet—just like my father. I've never been able to—'

Tiarnan turned and pulled her into his arms, and Kate shut up instantly at the feel of his body so close to hers, one hand low on her back and the other held high. She could feel Tiarnan's hips move sinuously against hers, his legs making hers move in tandem with his.

His voice came low near her ear, making her tingle, 'Just feel the beat—let it go through you.'

All Kate felt was boneless, with an indecent need running through her.

Tiarnan moved them apart and put both hands on her hips. 'See? Look at my feet. Copy what I'm doing.'

She could barely function. Tiarnan's broad chest and those lean hips were hypnotising her. She didn't know if what she was doing was anything like dancing, but she did feel the deeply sexy beat in her blood, and when Tiarnan turned her around and pulled her back against him, his arm across her midriff, she didn't even care that she couldn't dance. She had to close her eyes and try not to let out a low moan of pleasure.

Then the music changed again to slow and sexy. Tiarnan twirled her around with effortless ease and pulled her into him, so close that she could feel the imprint of his body all along hers. He tipped up her chin. Her head fell back.

'See? Anyone can dance.'

'I wouldn't go that far,' Kate said huskily, her eyes seemingly riveted to Tiarnan's mouth, and as if to prove her point she stumbled and stood on his foot. She looked up to see him wince slightly and smiled sweetly. 'See?'

'It'll take a lot more than standing on my foot to diminish this.'

His voice was low and dark with promise as he pulled her even closer, and Kate's eyes widened on his when she felt the hard thrust of his arousal just above the apex of her legs. The silk of her dress was no barrier to the size and strength of it.

Hot liquid seemed to pool southwards in answer to his body's calling. Her hand clenched on his shoulder, as if to stop herself falling.

'See?' he asked mockingly, his smile dangerous with sensual intent.

Kate could barely hold it together. A bone-deep tremor was starting to build up through her whole body. She felt Tiarnan's hand go to her neck, massaging the delicate skin, undoing her hair so that it fell down her back. A shudder of pure desire ran through her, making her move instinctively against him, eliciting a deep growl from his throat. She turned her face into his neck, her hand resting on the hair at the back of his collar. He brought their joined hands in close to his chest. Her lips were so close to his hot skin. The slightly musky smell was an overwhelming temptation to snake out her tongue and taste, just for a second. She could feel the kick of his pulse under her tongue and exhilaration fired her blood.

Tiarnan stopped dead on the middle of the dance floor and pulled her even closer, urgency in his movements. 'Let's get out of here.'

Kate could do nothing but nod silently. Now she knew she was ready. Now she knew that nothing could hold her back.

Everything happened quickly. The smiling driver took them home. Tiarnan took her by the hand and led her into the house and up the stairs. One or two dim lights lit the way.

All Kate was aware of was the burning need inside her, the prospect of fulfilment more heady than anything she'd ever known. Since the moment she'd stepped up to Tiarnan to kiss him boldly on the lips all those years ago it had never been enough.

So now, when he halted outside her bedroom door and turned to face her, saying with a low voice, 'Kate, I want you. But I'll wait if I—' It was the easiest thing in the world to step close and put a finger to his lips.

'So have me...I'm yours.' She couldn't play games, couldn't

deny the need that had given her the impetus to say yes to coming here. She'd been waiting for this moment for so long.

Tiarnan emitted a guttural sound of satisfaction and pulled her in so tight against him she didn't know if it was his heart-beat or hers she could feel thumping so loudly and heavily. His mouth seemed to hover over hers for a long moment, as if re-lishing the anticipation, the moment, and then, with one hand spearing her hair possessively, his mouth slanted down onto hers, and Kate gave herself up to the maelstrom that erupted instantly around them.

Without really knowing how they'd got there, Kate found herself standing in Tiarnan's bedroom, facing him. Both were breathing harshly. Her universe had contracted to this moment and this man. It felt utterly right, as necessary as breathing.

She held her half-removed dress to her chest, not even knowing how it had become undone, and with a deep ragged breath let it go. It pooled at her feet in a swirl of vibrant blue silk. She kicked off her shoes and stood before Tiarnan in nothing but lace pants.

'Come here,' he said throatily.

Kate moved forward and started to undo his shirt, fingers grazing and revealing dark olive skin covered in a smattering of dark hair. He was so masculine, and it resonated with something deep within her. Recognition of a mate. Her belly quivered. He hadn't touched her yet, and it was all the more erotic for that. Her breasts felt full and aching and tight, the tips tingling pain-fully. Kate pushed his shirt off his shoulders and down his arms, and it too joined her dress in a pool of white on the floor.

She trailed her hands down across his defined pectorals, felt his indrawn sharp breath as her fingers trailed lower. She looked down, and amidst the haze of heat that seemed to surround them saw the small cut where her knitting needle had stabbed him just a few nights ago. She traced it lightly, and then bent forward to press a soft kiss to it.

Tiarnan sucked in a breath at the feel of her lips and her breath there. Her hair fell over one shoulder, and when she stood again he looked greedily at her lush form in all its glory. The tiny waist, feminine hips, impossibly long legs…up again to surprisingly full breasts. He quite literally ached to touch her, but this sweet anticipation was too exquisite.

With a voice he barely recognised as his own because it was so full of raw need, he said, 'Undress me. Please.'

Kate looked up into Tiarnan's face. She read the restraint and silently thanked him for it. He was giving her time, letting her dictate the pace. Yet she knew if he threw her on the bed right now and took her with no further ado she'd be ready. She felt indecently damp between her thighs. With other men since Tiarnan she'd always felt self-conscious, awkward, but with him it felt natural, *right,* and that gave her confidence. She had the fleeting wish that she could eradicate all other experiences and make this moment her first time all over again…

Feeling unbearably emotional for a second, she stepped forward and reached up to put her arms around his neck, bringing her breasts into contact with his chest. A shudder of reaction ran through both of them, and it took all of Kate's strength to stay standing and say somewhat shakily, belying her outward show of confidence, 'I'll undress you—but first…a kiss.'

Tiarnan couldn't resist. He smoothed his hands over her slender arms, then down over the bare curve of her waist and hips, settling on her behind, drawing her close. He dipped his head and met Kate's mouth with his, and within seconds the flames of desire were igniting around them, their tongues dancing feverishly. Kate forgot about teasing and restraint. She strained upwards on tiptoe to try and get even closer, pressing herself against Tiarnan blindly, seeking more, seeking to assuage the urgent need building deep in her core.

Without breaking contact she brought her hands down between them to his trousers, found the opening, careless in her haste, dragging his trousers down impatiently over lean hips. His hands had gone under her panties, moulding the cheeks of her bottom, making her arch into him, thwarting her attempts to drag down his trousers.

'Tiarnan...' She almost sobbed with frustration, not even sure what was hampering her, only knowing that she didn't want to stop touching him for a second. To lose contact with that hot skin, that heavenly musky scent, would be like depriving herself of oxygen.

His hands came up to her arms and put her back slightly. She felt dizzy, and they were both breathing as if they'd just been running.

'Kate...' He sounded hoarse, surprised and slightly bewildered. 'How could I have denied myself this for so long...?'

With indecent haste he brought his hands to his trousers and finished what Kate couldn't do. Finally he stood before her, naked and proud, virility oozing from every pore. Kate looked down and her throat went dry as she took him in in all his glory. She looked up again, and even though the room was dark she could see the expression on his face, the look in his darkened eyes. Passion and desire blazed forth—*for her.*

She was feeling suddenly weak, and as if he sensed it Tiarnan took her hand and led her over to the bed, through the muslin curtains that had been drawn down to protect against the stinging night insects. Surrounded by the gauzy material, the bed was like a cocoon, an oasis of pleasure.

Kate lay back and watched as Tiarnan stretched over her. He smoothed back her hair and it felt unbearably tender. Then he looked down her body, and wherever his eyes rested seemed to throb in response. He cupped one breast and Kate arched her back, eyes widening in a mute plea. She heard a dark chuckle, and felt his breath feather on her hot skin before he took the turgid tip into his mouth and suckled mercilessly, inciting the most intense response Kate could ever remember. She was gasping, grabbing his shoulders, his arms, hands clenched tight around bulging hard muscles as his mouth moved from one breast to the other, torturing her with pleasure. And then he moved down, and down again. The breeze whispered over the wet tips of her breasts and her stomach, where his tongue had touched her.

He pulled down her pants, throwing them aside, and then with ruthless intent pulled her legs apart. Kate stopped breathing for a long moment, her belly sucked in as she watched Tiarnan looking at her with such intimacy that she almost couldn't stand it.

Rising desire drowned out her mortification. Instinctively she moved on the bed, hips lifting slightly. 'Please...' She wasn't even sure what she was asking for.

Tiarnan looked at her, his hands travelling back up her legs, coming ever closer to her centre, thumbs massaging the tender inner skin of her thighs. His hands stopped at the very top of her legs, thumbs resting on the curls that covered her. They started moving slowly, back and forth, seeking, exploring, kneading her flesh.

Kate sucked in a breath that felt like a sob. *'Tiarnan.'*

'What? Tell me what you want?'

As if it was the easiest thing in the world.

'I...' Kate began brokenly. 'I want you to touch me... I want you inside me...'

One hand moved, and Kate felt long fingers thread through the damp curls, exploring ever inwards until he felt her slick heat for himself. She felt his reaction run through him. His erection lay thick and heavy against her thigh. She moved restlessly.

'Like this? First I touch...'

And he did. He touched her intimately. Fingers moving in and out, testing her, drawing out her response, his thumb finding that small hard nub and massaging it until Kate's hands clenched in the bedsheets so tight that her knuckles were white.

She felt all at once helpless, wanton and insatiable. And mortified at how he was turning her into someone she didn't even recognise. He bent his head, his chest close to hers, brushing against sensitive breasts, and kissed her deeply, erotically, as his hand and fingers caressed her intimately.

But just as she could feel the elusive peak she'd rarely reached with anyone else come like a vision through the haze of desire Tiarnan broke the kiss and removed his hand.

'Now *you* touch…'

He brought her hand down to cover his shaft. Kate's eyes grew big and round, glued to his as she allowed herself to feel and explore as he had done. It was his turn to shift restlessly, colour slashing his cheeks as she moved her hand, tightened her grip, feeling the satin smooth skin slip up and down over the steel-hard core. She could feel their heartbeats thudding slowly and heavily.

When he looked down at her with tense jaw and fever-bright eyes she took her hand away, and shifted herself so that she lay under him. She spread her legs, opening herself up to his welcome heat and heaviness.

'Now… I want you…' She reached up and pressed a hot kiss to his mouth, her tongue slipping inside with seductive innocence for a moment before she said, '…inside me.'

Tiarnan had lost all sense of time and place. At the last second before desire sucked him under completely he reached for protection and smoothed it on with all the finesse of a novice. This scene was so reminiscent of a dream he hadn't even acknowledged. He could feel Kate move beneath him. Her hair was spread in a golden halo around her head, and her eyes, like two huge pools of blue, looked up at him. Her legs parted a fraction more, and because it was the most necessary thing in the world he slid his erection, which felt engorged to the point of pain, into her silken heat, and died a small death of pleasure at the exquisite sensation.

He felt her move her hips, drawing him deeper. Exerting extreme control, he slowly started to thrust in and out. His eyes were locked on hers. Twin flags of colour stained her cheeks, her lips were plump and red…her teeth bit them as she fought to keep her moans back. It was all Tiarnan could do not to explode there and then. Seeing her like this was a fulfilment of something he'd so long suppressed.

Their skin was slick with sweat, their heartbeats no longer slow and heavy but frantic. The tempo increased. Tiarnan could feel Kate's legs wrap around him, urging him even deeper, harder. The pinnacle came in a blaze of white light and pleasure so intense they both stopped breathing for a long moment, hung suspended in time. And then came the fall, tumbling down and down all the way, their bodies releasing and pulsing for an age as Kate accepted Tiarnan's weight onto her, wrapped legs and arms around him even tighter, binding him to her.

Tiarnan woke at some point and felt an empty space beside him. Immediately a low hum of panic gripped him that he did not like. He lifted his head. Dawn was touching the sky outside and Kate stood on the balcony, leaning on the railing looking out to sea, dressed in nothing but his white shirt. The outline of her body was silhouetted enticingly under the material. Relief surged through him—which he also did not like.

Tiarnan got out of bed. As if linked to him by an invisible thread, Kate stood and turned around, pulled the shirt together over her chest haphazardly with one hand. Her hair was tumbled around her shoulders. Tiarnan prowled towards her. She was the only thing filling his mind, his vision in that moment. Seeing her dressed in nothing but his white shirt should have been a cliché. But it wasn't. Plenty of women had dressed like this for him, as if in an effort to do the contrived sexy thing, and all it had incited within him was mild irritation. Right now, though, irritation was the last thing he was feeling.

What he was feeling was a surge of primal possessiveness rushing through him.

Kate stood straighter as he came closer, put her hands out behind her on the railing. The shirt fell open, revealing tantalising glimpses of the twin globes of her breasts and then, down further, the ever so soft swell of her belly and the apex of her thighs, where golden curls hid paradise. Tiarnan reached her and pulled her into him, his arms around her naked back under the shirt. Even though they'd barely slept all night, he was ready to take her again.

He felt her lift one leg to hook it around his hip...knew instantly that she was ready again too. It was the most powerful aphrodisiac. They didn't even make it back to the bed. Tiarnan slid into her there and then. And with the dawn breaking somewhere in the east, tingeing the sky with pink, he and Kate entered another realm of the senses.

CHAPTER SEVEN

KATE had never felt so lethargic in her life—as if every limb was weighted down with a delicious warm stone. She couldn't even open her eyes. Vague flashes of memory came back: her dress pooling at her feet; kissing Tiarnan until she had to break away to suck in air; his body moving into hers, taking her breath away all over again, slippery with sweat; Tiarnan drawing her on top of him and watching her face as she took him in, then flipping her onto her back, driving in and out with such exquisite and ruthless precision that she'd been begging for release, near to tears.

Kate tried without success to shut the images out. Heat was already flaring through her just thinking about what they'd shared. She remembered getting up at some point and standing on the balcony, as if to try and make sense of it all, and then she'd heard him get up and he'd joined her there. Within seconds of touching they'd been burning up all over again. She squeezed her eyes shut tight, as if that might block out the wanton image. She could vaguely remember him lifting her up into his arms…after that a bath…and then oblivion. An oblivion touched with the peace that came from a long-held desire finally fulfilled. Her somewhat pathetic concern that sleeping with Tiarnan might prove to be disappointing had been blown into the stratosphere.

Just then a sound came from somewhere near—a door opened, small feet ran in.

'Katie, Katie—come on, get up, sleepyhead!'

Immediately she was alert. She was in her own bed, dressed in the T-shirt and boxer shorts she'd laid out on her pillow the previous evening. Rosie and her friend Zoe were standing looking at her, holding back the muslin curtain that was around the bed. Kate sat up and pushed down the clamour of questions. Tiarnan must have put her to bed here and dressed her after the bath. Had she really been so exhausted that she hadn't even been aware?

Heat suffused her face, and she tried to hide it by throwing back the covers and climbing out of bed. She smiled at the girls, hoping they wouldn't notice her discomfiture.

'What time is it?'

Rosie rolled her eyes at her friend, who giggled shyly. They were both dressed in shorts and vest tops, feet bare. Kate could see a trickle of sand had followed them into the room.

'It's *really* late, Katie. Nearly midday! Come on—we're going to the beach. Tiarnan wouldn't let us wake you for ages. He said you were jet-lagged…'

The two girls ran out of the room again, shouting that they'd see her downstairs in ten minutes. Kate sagged back onto the bed and pushed her hand through her hair. The thought of seeing Tiarnan after last night made her tummy flip. Was it even real? Or had she dreamt it? But her body was the evidence. She was glad he'd had the foresight to put her into her own bed. She'd obviously been barely capable of moving. The fact that *he'd* managed to retain a cool measure of control and was clearly marking the boundaries between them made her feel vulnerable.

As she stood under the spray of her shower a few minutes later, Kate's movements suddenly halted. She remembered that moment on the balcony; they hadn't used protection. Tiarnan had been so careful to protect them up to that point, and she hadn't missed the horrorstruck look on his face when he'd realised. The pain of seeing how violently he'd castigated himself had led her to reassure him quickly that it would be fine—she was at a safe stage in her cycle. And she *was*. But still, it shocked her how easily they'd been careless, and he'd vowed vociferously to make sure it didn't happen again. She had no desire either, to risk bringing a child into a very temporary moment of madness. And the thought of what such a scenario would mean to Tiarnan made her go cold.

'Morning. Or should I say *afternoon?*'

Kate took a deep breath to steady herself against the bone-tingling effect of the deep, sexy drawling voice before she looked up from tying her flat sandals, sitting on the bottom stair. But she couldn't stop her heart beating wildly. Mortification twisted her insides anew as the enormity of what had happened hit her. She'd been so easy. She'd shown him with bells on how she'd hungered for him for years... She should try to hide that vulnerability from him. She had to somehow make him think he was just another in a long line of lovers. She had to protect herself from him.

Gathering all her training, that armour she'd perfected over the years, she looked up and steeled herself not to react to seeing him—but it was hard. He stood leaning nonchalantly against a doorjamb, dressed in a white T-shirt that strained across the biceps of his arms and faded loose khaki shorts. Battered sneakers on his feet.

She finished fiddling with her sandals and stood, self-conscious even though she was dressed similarly, in long shorts and a vest top. Perfectly respectable. She saw that they were alone and came close to him. Trying not to falter, she tipped her face up to his and said, *sotto voce,* 'Thanks for last night, I really enjoyed it.'

She saw his smile fade ever so slightly. A hard gleam came into his eyes and she wanted to gag. Those words were so meaningless, when she really wanted to say that the previous night had been the most exquisite experience of her existence. That she'd already stored away every single moment in her memory. But she had to remember who she was dealing with—*had to*. Or he'd destroy her.

He took her hand before she knew what he was doing and raised it to his mouth, pressing a kiss to the underside of her wrist, causing heat to flood her belly and her breath to catch.

'I enjoyed it too. I'm already looking forward to tonight.'

Kate's eyes were snared by his. She was terrified that he would see that she was putting on a desperate act. She smiled and it felt brittle. She could do this if she had to.

'Me too.'

Just then sounds came from outside, and they moved apart just as Rosie burst into the hall. 'Come *on*, you guys. We'll be late!'

Tiarnan bent down to pick up a big basket that seemed to be bursting at the seams.

'Where are we going?' Kate asked as Rosie hopped around, impatient to go.

Mama Lucille came into the hall then, wiping her hands on an apron, and dragged Rosie close for a big hug and kiss.

Tiarnan looked back at Kate as he dodged around Rosie and Mama Lucille. 'We're going to the beach with a picnic. Zoe's family will be there too.'

Kate followed them out to the Jeep, which was laden down with things. This was obviously a bit of a ritual for them, and she realised belatedly that it was Sunday. It must be a traditional family day out for the locals.

Mama Lucille surprised Kate by giving her a big expansive hug too, and then they set off, the two giggling girls in the back reminding Kate bittersweetly of herself and Sorcha when they'd been young.

Disconcertingly, as if able to read her mind, Tiarnan said while gesturing to the back, 'Remind you of anyone?'

Kate smiled. 'I was just thinking about that.'

'Thinking about what?' Rosie piped up from the back, proving that her ears were very keen.

Kate and Tiarnan shared a complicit smile, and Kate couldn't stop her heart feeling as if it was about to burst. But she turned around and started to tell the two girls stories about her and Sorcha when they'd been young.

That evening, when they were in a very bedraggled and sandy Jeep returning home as night fell, Kate knew she hadn't enjoyed a day so much in ages. She felt deliciously sunburned, her skin tingling in the aftermath of a day spent outdoors. They'd gone to a beach that was obviously a local secret as it had been empty but for them and Zoe's extended family, all Mama Lucille's children and grandchildren, nieces and nephews. She could see what Tiarnan meant. Rosie was as much a part of that family as their own kids—she could even see that there was a fragile and gradual thawing in Rosie and Tiarnan's relationship. She hoped that the holiday would prove to give Tiarnan the breakthrough he sought with Rosie.

Earlier in the day Kate had given up trying to keep track of everyone she'd been introduced to, and Zoe's mother Anne-Marie had taken her under her wing. She was a beautiful woman in her early thirties, who had three children including Zoe, the eldest.

They'd been watching an impromptu football game, with everyone chaotically involved, toddlers and all in the mix, when Kate had impulsively confided, 'I envy you.'

Anne-Marie had looked shocked. 'Are you mad? You'd give up a glamorous lifestyle travelling around the world to live with *this* kind of mayhem?'

But the other woman's sparkling eyes had told another story. Kate had felt her heart clench. She'd hidden the true extent of her desire to get out of modelling and settle down even from Sorcha. Somehow here, with this woman who was little more than a stranger, it had been easy to smile wryly and say with feeling, 'In a heartbeat.'

Anne-Marie had leant close then, and said conspiratorially, 'He's a good man.'

Kate had blushed immediately and realised to her horror that her eyes had been greedily following Tiarnan as he'd run bare-chested down the beach with the ball, a gaggle of children running after him, adults laughing. It was a world away from the austere image he projected to the world of finance and high-powered achieving. In truth, she was slightly shocked to see this side of him—and shocked at the feeling it caused deep inside her. A deep yearning for family, *love,* for belonging. With him. When she should be getting over him…

Kate tried to be cool. 'Oh, I've known Tiarnan for years. His sister Sorcha's my best friend. And, yes, he *is* a good man.'

Anne-Marie hadn't looked fooled for a second. She'd just said, 'He's never brought anyone else here, you know…and no man is an island.'

Kate's face had been burning by then, but thankfully Anne-Marie had deftly defused the situation and stood, reaching down to haul Kate up too.

'Come on—let's show the men a thing or two.'

Kate's attention returned to the present. It was just the three of them in the Jeep—Rosie sleepy in the back, Tiarnan driving. She snuck a look at his proud profile as he drove. Anne-Marie was wrong, Tiarnan most certainly *was* an island, and there was no room on it for her except as a temporary bed companion. The sooner she could come to terms with that, the better.

After dinner Kate offered to go and see if Rosie was tucked into bed. Tiarnan caught her hand to pull her back and said with a se-ductive drawl, 'I didn't bring you here to act as a nanny to Rosie.'

Kate looked down at him and her heart twisted. They'd all showered and changed as soon as they'd got back, and Tiarnan looked heart-stoppingly handsome with damp hair, in a clean shirt and worn jeans. His blue eyes were even more intense against the slight tan he'd already acquired in one day.

She pulled her hand free. 'Don't worry. I know exactly why I'm here, Tiarnan. We both do.'

Something in her voice or expression caught him and caused an ache in the region of his chest, but he had no idea why. He watched her walk out, her sexy cut-off shorts effortlessly show-casing her long lissom legs. She wore a peasant-style top and her hair was loose down her back, slightly darker as it was still a little damp. Her scent hovered on the air and he had to fight not to close his eyes and savour it.

Slightly irritated with himself for this moonstruck streak he wasn't used to, he turned back to the table and drank down the rest of his wine. Along with the heat of desire that washed through him in waves was a much more ambiguous feeling.

He'd expected Kate to suffer somewhat through the day, having to spend it *en famille*. But she had smiled and gelled with everyone immediately. She'd seemed to genuinely enjoy herself—and the rambunctious nature of Mama Lucille's family. He'd seen her talking to Anne-Marie, laughing easily, as if they'd known each other for years.

She'd been quite happy to muck in and help out with the food and children too, assuming a natural gentle authority which had taken him by surprise. When they'd been playing football he'd seen her go to pick up one of the smaller children who'd been accidentally knocked over without a moment's hesitation, and even though she didn't even know him, she'd hugged him close and kissed him better, so that by the time the father had rushed over the child had been clinging to Kate and playing happily with her blonde hair.

As if to distract his line of thinking from going down a dangerous path he had no desire to explore, he recalled her body in its petrol blue bikini. The other men had had the nous not to stop and stare, but he'd been aware of their interest when she'd first stripped off to go into the water with Rosie and Zoe and the others. Immediately he'd irrationally regretted bringing her with them, and not locking her up in the house or back in his home in Madrid. And yet her bikini had been no more or less revealing than Anne-Marie's, or any of the other women's...

Despite that, he could recall only too easily his intense relief when she'd put on her shorts and top again to come and play football. He'd been afraid that he wouldn't have the restraint not to insist that she cover up. He rationalised it: having slept with her only the night before, after such a long build-up, his desire still felt raw. He was just realising how hard it was to share her with everyone else so soon.

The lingering traces of that desire were making him hard again. He'd spent the day in a perpetual state of near arousal, taking frequent swims to disguise it. And he couldn't block out or forget that he'd been so hot for her last night, that for the first time in his life *ever,* he'd forgotten about protection. He hadn't even been careless with Stella Rios. She'd assured him she'd been on the pill, and even knowing that he'd insisted on using protection. But one time it had broken, and *that* had been her chance for convincing him he might be Rosie's father—especially after she'd revealed that she'd lied about taking the pill...

Tiarnan assured himself now that Kate was *not* Stella Rios. He would not be caught again. He forced himself to relax, and waited to hear her footfall coming back downstairs. He couldn't help thinking of that indecipherable expression that had flashed in her eyes just now, and her behaviour today. Most of the women he'd sought out for affairs in the past would have been clinging to him like a limpet, complaining vociferously about the rustic nature of the entertainment. Quite apart from the fact that he had to concede that he wouldn't have brought them here in the first place.

A feeling of vulnerability swamped him. Was he allowing Kate to play him? In a way that no other woman had done before? Not even Stella Rios?

Enough! Tiarnan chastised himself for his introspection. They were effectively alone again, and he could spend the night punishing her for making him feel so uncharacteristically vulnerable. He heard her coming back down the stairs and stood jerkily, his usual grace deserting him as he turned and went to meet her halfway...

Two days later Kate sat in the shade in the garden, knitting. No sound warned her she wasn't alone, so when she heard a softly drawled, 'I come in peace; I'm not armed,' she nearly jumped out of her skin. She looked up to see Tiarnan standing there, his hands up in a comic gesture of surrender, looking expressively at her knitting.

He'd taken her by surprise in more ways than one because, predictably, he'd been occupying her thoughts. In particular, vivid images of last night in his bed, and the moments of ecstasy she'd experienced in his arms. She felt as though he'd be able to see that straight away and looked down again, feeling cross, putting the knitting away.

'Don't worry—I'll restrain myself.' She knew she must sound cool. But it was the only way she could stem this constant state of heat she seemed to be in. Escaping for quiet moments was keeping her semi-sane. And she was also consciously trying to give Tiarnan time alone with Rosie.

He came and sat down in the wicker lounger chair beside her, long bare legs stretched out, making her eyes drop betrayingly to linger on their perfectly formed muscles. She couldn't help but remember how it felt to have those strong hair-roughened thighs between her own, and a quiver of heat made her clench her legs together. He was wearing his usual Martinique uniform of casual shorts and T-shirt, looking as relaxed as any local. Whereas she felt as tightly wound as a spring.

'I thought Rosie was with you?' Kate said, as much to know as in an effort to fill the silence.

Tiarnan had put his head back and closed his eyes. The dappled sunlight coming through the leaves of the tree above them caught his skin in patches. He was looking more tanned by the day, and with it more devilishly handsome.

He opened his eyes and looked at her, shaking his head, putting his arms behind it to cushion it. Supremely relaxed. 'She went into town to go shopping with Papa Joe.'

'Zoe…?'

He shook his head again. 'They're still in school here, so Rosie has to do without her partner in crime during the day.'

'Oh…' Kate felt unaccountably awkward. She still hadn't got used to dealing with Tiarnan during the day, after nights which were filled with such passion. She was slightly overwhelmed. And, if she was honest, she was afraid of spending too much time with him, getting closer, seeing even more aspects of his fascinating character.

He leant forward and reached out a hand. Kate looked at it suspiciously.

'Come for a drive with me. I want to show you something.'

Tiarnan could see the reluctance on Kate's face and irritation spiked through him. She'd been keeping her distance the past couple of days and he didn't like it. During the night she was undeniably his—more passionate than anything he'd ever experienced. But apart from that… It was as if there were two different Kates. She gave off an air of insouciance he knew and expected. And yet she wasn't constantly seeking his attention or moaning about the lack of civilisation. She was here knitting quietly in the garden. As much as he hated this compulsion to get to know her better, he couldn't ignore it. He hungered for her, and he realised now that he hungered just to spend time with her—a novel desire, and one that didn't sit entirely well with him.

'What about Rosie? Won't she be home soon?'

Tiarnan shook his head. 'Papa Joe is taking her over to the other side of the island afterwards to a market. They'll eat there and won't be back till late. Rosie's been to the place I want to take you a hundred times already. Come on, Kate. Or are you going to tell me that knitting is more exciting than taking a mystery tour with me?'

He quirked a brow. Kate's insides liquefied. How could she resist this man? She made a show of seriously contemplating for a moment whether she'd prefer to sit and knit the day away, and squealed when Tiarnan moved like lightning and put her over his shoulder, lifting her as if she weighed no more than a bag of sugar. She was wearing a relatively short sundress, and his warm hand was disturbingly close to the tops of her bare thighs and her bottom.

'Tiarnan Quinn—put me down this instant! What if someone sees us? Mama Lucille…'

She felt Tiarnan swat her bottom playfully and say loudly, 'Mama Lucille has seen plenty in her lifetime—haven't you, Mama? I'm taking Kate out for the afternoon. Don't worry about dinner for us.'

Kate's face burned and her fists clenched when she heard the familiar full-bodied chuckle and saw Mama Lucille's feet in their flip-flops pass them by.

She spied something out of the corner of her eye, put out a hand. 'Wait! My camera.'

Tiarnan obediently halted and retraced his steps, picking up Kate's camera which lay on a hall table. Then they were out through the front door and down to the Jeep, where he deposited Kate in the passenger seat with surprising gentleness. He handed her her camera before coming around and getting into the driver's seat.

They were pulling away from the villa within seconds, and Kate couldn't help a bubble of excitement rising within her. Tiarnan looked at her and smiled, and it was so carefree that she couldn't help but smile back. Her armour and her resistance were melting in a pool at her feet and there was nothing she could do to stop it.

She sat back in the seat and said mock-sulkily, 'I was quite happy knitting quietly, you know. This is meant to be a holiday.'

For a second Tiarnan had to reconcile that image of such domesticity with the woman he'd expected Kate to be. It was an anomaly he ruthlessly diverted his attention away from.

'I'm sure...' he said then, slanting her a mischievous look. 'I could see how fast you were knitting—feverishly, one could say, almost as if your mind was filled not with thoughts of casting on and single back cross stitches, but rather something more...elemental...'

Kate burned—because he was absolutely right. Though she didn't know what was more shocking—that or the fact that he knew any knitting terminology.

She turned to face him in her seat. The sea was an amazing backdrop behind him. 'Don't tell me you've had to put up with *other* women being more enthralled with knitting than you?' She opened her eyes wide, acting innocent.

He shook his head. 'You're on your own there, Kate Lancaster. No, it was my mother. You don't remember all those hideous Christmas jumpers we got every year, until Sorcha was discovered giving hers away to a homeless person?'

Kate laughed out loud. 'How could I have forgotten? Your poor mother was so insulted—and if I remember it had a lovely holly and mistletoe pattern, which I must say in her defence would not have been easy to do...'

Tiarnan smiled ruefully. 'I'm sure. I was just relieved that

Sorcha had unwittingly saved us from a lifetime of lurid Christmas jumpers.'

Kate was tempted to return with a quip that *she* could fill that gaping hole in his life, but stopped abruptly when she realised how it might sound. As if she expected to be a part of his life after this holiday was over.

He looked at her curiously, and she could feel that she'd gone slightly pale. 'What is it?'

She shook her head and smiled brightly. 'Nothing. Nothing at all. So—where exactly are you taking me?'

'Ah, that's for me to know and you to see.' He glanced at the camera nestled on her lap, her hands over it protectively. 'That looks pretty professional. I saw you taking pictures in the garden earlier…'

Kate lifted up the camera and looked at it. She felt self-conscious.

'The photographers at work told me which one I should buy if I was seriously interested in learning.'

'And are you? Seriously interested?'

Kate shrugged one slim shoulder. 'I've done some photography courses. Travelling around the world so much I get to see so many things, and I wanted to start documenting them… It's a hobby, I guess you could say.'

Tiarnan cast her a look. She was avoiding his eye, studying the camera. He guessed intuitively that she must be very good. She seemed to have the kind of personality that would be utterly respectful of anything or anyone she wanted to photograph.

They drove on in silence for a bit, and eventually Kate read out the name of the town they'd come into, where Tiarnan started slowing down.

'Saint-Pierre…'

Tiarnan stopped the Jeep and parked up, and they got out. He immediately came and took Kate's hand. She didn't pull away, and a surge of something went through him.

Her hand felt so good in Tiarnan's. She loved the way he was so tactile. With other men when they'd tried to maintain contact she'd always felt uncomfortable. She looked around curiously at the streets. It was a pretty enough town, but...

'What are you thinking?' Tiarnan looked at her intently.

Kate stood still. 'I don't know,' she answered after a long moment. 'It's weird. It's almost as if the buildings don't fit the town, or something...' A shiver went down her spine. 'And there's something eerie about it too...'

Tiarnan pointed at a mountain in the distance. 'See that?'

Kate nodded.

'That's Mount Pelée. In 1902 it erupted, and within minutes this town and its thirty thousand or so inhabitants were decimated. The only survivor was a man who was locked in a prison cell below ground.'

'Those poor people,' Kate breathed, and then looked at Tiarnan. 'It's almost inconceivable to imagine.'

He nodded, and noticed that she was shading her eyes from the sun with her hand. He felt a dart of guilt. He'd rushed her out of the house so fast she hadn't had time to pick anything up. He spied a shop across the road and led her there.

Two minutes later they emerged, and Tiarnan handed Kate a pair of lurid pink sunglasses, complete with pineapples on each corner, and a big floppy straw hat with a ring of fake flowers around the base.

She sighed and took them from him. 'Just what I've always wanted. To look like a clown.'

But she took them and put them on, and smiled up at him so beautifully that he couldn't resist taking her face in his hands and pressing a kiss to her lips. Only when someone wolf-whistled nearby did he let her go, slightly in shock at how turned-on he was already—and how easy it had been to kiss her like that when he normally had an absolute abhorrence for public displays of affection. He took her by the hand and led her away.

Kate's heart was beating quickly in her chest as she held onto the ridiculous hat and followed Tiarnan. That kiss had been so impromptu and so devastating. He'd taken her completely by surprise, buying the hat and glasses too. Right then she wouldn't have wanted their designer equivalent in a million years.

They walked for a bit, then came to the local museum where Tiarnan showed her the exhibits. Outside in the car park they looked down over the town. It was obvious where the lines of destruction still lay, despite the new buildings and life going on.

It gave Kate a sense of how fragile life was—how quickly everything could be ripped away. She felt as though she were falling off a high precipice. Unconsciously she gripped Tiarnan's hand tighter and he turned to look at her,

'OK?'

Kate tried to drive down the overwhelming sense of making every moment count with this man, because she knew now it would be all that she had, and she turned and looked up, pasting on a bland smile. 'You certainly know how to show a girl a good uplifting time.'

He smiled dangerously and drew her into him tightly. Kate held in a gasp at the potent feel of his rock-solid body against hers. The other tourists milling around them were forgotten.

'We'll discuss good uplifting times when we get home.'

'Promises, promises,' Kate said somewhat shakily, and Tiarnan let her go again, but kept a hold of her hand.

Later, eating ice creams he'd bought them outside a shop, they walked back to the Jeep. They stopped near the harbour wall for a moment, to finish eating, and something in Tiarnan's stance caught Kate's eye. He was looking out to sea, his profile so beautiful that she couldn't resist lifting her camera and taking a quick snap. He turned when he heard the shutter click and Kate smiled. 'For posterity,' she said. And felt inordinately guilty—because she knew it would be for *her*.

* * *

They took the road back the way they'd come, returning south, and Kate felt acutely aware of *everything*. Tiarnan turned left off the main road at one point and all of a sudden they seemed to be in the middle of a lush rainforest. Kate put out her hand as they drove, to try and touch the branches by the side of the road.

'This is so beautiful. I'd never have imagined this kind of scenery here.'

'Wait till you see what's up here…'

Kate felt a bubble of pure joy rise upwards within her as she watched Tiarnan drive against this backdrop. She was truly content, for the first time in a long time, and she wouldn't allow thoughts of the end of this holiday, and inevitably this affair, to cloud the moment.

They pulled up outside an impressive church and Tiarnan said, 'Remind you of anything?'

Kate looked up and gasped. 'It's the Sacré-Coeur!'

'A replica,' Tiarnan confirmed, and got out. 'Come on—there are some amazing views over Forte-de-France below…'

A short while later, as they drove back towards the coast, Kate's head was bursting with images—and a lingering sense of peace from the church that had been built as a smaller replica of the iconic Parisian landmark.

She could recognise the route now. They weren't too far from home. But Tiarnan surprised her by taking a winding road down towards the sea, and pulling in outside a beautiful old colonial-style house, half buried in thick bougainvillaea and hibiscus flowers. Martinique was certainly living up to its name as 'the isle of flowers'.

It turned out that the house was actually a converted restaurant, and when they walked in Kate wasn't surprised to see Tiarnan greeted like an old friend. As was the custom she was getting used to, she was greeted effusively, and they were led to a stunning white-clothed table in a wrought-iron balconied alcove that looked directly out to the sea and the setting sun.

Kate leant forward, a small frown creasing her forehead. 'Aren't we dressed a little…well, casually for somewhere like this?'

Tiarnan looked around then, and noticed a few men sitting with partners and looking at Kate with brazen appreciation. Jealousy rose swiftly. He turned back to Kate. She looked all at once so demure and so incredibly sexy that he had to bite back a completely irrational urge to tell her to cover up. And how could she, when he'd all but manhandled her out of the house earlier? Her hesitation before, in the garden, came back to him, made something inside him twist.

'You're fine,' he said gruffly.

She'd been a good sport today—happily wearing the ridiculous hat and glasses, taking snaps, eating ice cream at the side of the road. Once again he'd been hard pushed to think of any of his previous mistresses in those surroundings, happy to sightsee.

He gestured to her shoulders. 'You got a bit burnt today.'

Kate grimaced. 'Oh it's nothing.'

She looked at him with something almost like shyness in her expression, but Tiarnan had to reject that thought. It couldn't be. He wanted to keep seeing her as a cool, sophisticated woman of the world.

'It feels good, in all honesty. I usually have to be so careful of my skin. And my weight.' She rolled her eyes then, and imitated her agent's broad New York drawl.

'"Kate, honey, you're known for your porcelain skin. So don't gimme a heart attack and come back looking like me. I can take the sun. You can't. And whatever you do watch your weight. I'm always telling you, you don't have it as easy as the other girls, you're not naturally skinny. It's a shame, but we have our crosses to bear and yours is pasta…"'

She stopped and blushed when Tiarnan laughed out loud.

She knew he knew Maud well. She was Sorcha's agent too. Kate felt foolish all of a sudden. 'I'm sorry…Sorcha calls them my Maud monologues.'

He caught her hand, smiling widely. 'You mimic her brilliantly. I could have sworn she was here.'

Kate's hand tingled in his, and he only let go when a pristinely dressed waiter arrived and addressed Tiarnan in French while handing them menus.

Tiarnan replied fluently, and Kate made a face when the waiter left. 'No throwing of food allowed here, I'd guess?'

Tiarnan looked mock stern. 'Certainly not, young lady.'

Kate had to catch herself. She'd never have guessed she'd feel so at ease with Tiarnan, so comfortable. This day was in danger of becoming incredibly special, and she drove that thought down, to some deep and dark place. She took up the menu and made a great show of studying the indecipherable French.

After a long moment she heard an amused, 'Would you like me to translate?'

Drat the man. She had the grace to smile self-deprecatingly and put the menu down. 'Would you please?' she said. 'I don't particularly want frog's legs or snails.'

'So, the photography…tell me about it. Did you do a degree?'

Kate watched as Tiarnan speared a morsel of fish and ate it, and felt the familiar shame grip her. She nervously tucked her hair behind her ear.

'No…I couldn't do a degree because I never completed school…' She shrugged slightly and avoided his eye. 'I was already working in London and then New York…earning money…and then it was too late.'

She heard him put down his knife and fork. Compelled against her will, she met his eye.

'Kate, it's nothing to be ashamed of. I didn't go to college myself.'

She smiled tightly. 'Maybe, but in a world like this men are judged far less harshly than women if they've proved themselves in the interim—qualifications notwithstanding.'

He inclined his head and took a sip of wine. 'You're right. Unfortunately. But if it means that much to you why didn't you complete when you had a chance?'

'Like Sorcha, you mean?' Kate and Sorcha had both started modelling at the same time, but Sorcha had made the effort to get her Irish leaving certificate qualification, and had then had done a degree in psychology in New York.

Tiarnan nodded.

Kate shrugged again. How could she admit her even more secret shame, of constant years of her mother telling her that her looks were all that mattered and why should she worry about working? She took a fortifying sip of wine and looked at Tiarnan.

'You remember my mother?'

He nodded. He remembered a brash woman who had grated on his nerves—a woman who cared more for her appearance and her social standing than anything else. He also remembered that she would flirt outrageously with *him* at any given opportunity. He knew that on some level when Kate had approached him that night ten years ago he'd assumed she was of the same ilk as her mother—forward. And yet, despite her cool assurance after he'd put a stop to their lovemaking, he'd glimpsed a vulnerability that was at odds with her seemingly confident actions. He'd dismissed it that night and in the intervening years—especially as he witnessed her blooming into the stunning beauty she now was—and her cool exterior confirmed for him that she'd become accustomed to a certain kind of attention. But, despite all that, right now that vulnerability seemed to be back, and it jarred with his assessment of her character.

He tried to bring his focus back to the conversation, feeling as if he were treading on dangerous ground.

'How *is* your mother?'

Kate was glad to be stalled for a moment. She smiled tightly and looked at him. 'Oh, I'm sure she's fine. She's on a cruise with rich husband number four and blissfully happy, no doubt.'

Tiarnan frowned. 'You don't see her, then?'

Kate shook her head. 'Very infrequently. If she's shopping in New York for a few days or going to the shows… But in general she doesn't like to be reminded of her mortality, and I'm afraid that's what I do.'

Tiarnan winced inwardly. That didn't surprise him.

'My mother is a great believer in a woman surviving on her looks. After Sorcha and I were discovered by the model scout that day in Dublin she saw no real need for me to stay at school. I was never the most academic anyway, so in later years the thought of completing studies as an older student and failing was somewhat daunting.'

Tiarnan reached across and tipped up her chin from where she was studying the table. She felt excruciatingly exposed. She'd never admitted this to anyone. And now to *him* of all people? But with his hand on her chin she was forced to meet his gaze.

'Kate, you are most certainly not stupid, if that's what you're afraid of. You have an innate intelligence that anyone would recognise a mile away. And lack of qualifications hasn't stopped some of the world's most successful people from succeeding. I bet half the world-famous photographers you work with are self-taught.'

Kate gulped and reddened. Tiarnan had sounded almost angry.

As if he realised this, he took his hand away and said, 'Sorry…I just wouldn't want you to put yourself down like that.' He shook his head. 'Parents can be so cruel, and do so much damage.'

Kate felt a well of emotion rise up and had to blink away the prickling of tears. She put her hand over his and said huskily, 'Thank you for that. I know intellectually everything you say is right—and you're right about parents…' She smiled shakily, 'Rosie is lucky to have you for a father.'

He grimaced. 'You wouldn't think so at the moment. She goes out of her way to avoid me.'

Kate squeezed his hand. 'She'll come round. You'll see.'

Tiarnan just looked into the blue depths of Kate's eyes and felt unaccountably as if he were drowning.

That night when they returned to the villa Kate felt as though something had changed between her and Tiarnan. It felt dangerous. And yet heady.

She'd just come out of her bathroom, having washed her face, when Tiarnan appeared at her bedroom door. Her breath stalled in her throat and she felt her nipples respond with wanton eagerness. Aghast at her reaction, she reached for a wrap and pulled it on over her singlet and boxers, knowing it was slightly ridiculous to feel so self-conscious.

'Rosie wants to say goodnight to you.'

'Of course.'

Kate went to go out through the door, but Tiarnan blocked her way. His hands cupped her face and tipped it up, threading through her hair. He was huge, his shoulders blocking out the light, his face cast in shadow, and he looked so darkly handsome that Kate couldn't catch her breath again. Every part of her body reacted to his proximity.

'I enjoyed today, Kate—and this evening.'

'Me too,' she said huskily. The image of the sun setting over the sea beside them as they sipped wine and ate delicious food would be forever engraved on her memory.

He pressed the most fleeting and yet earth-shattering of kisses onto her mouth and said simply, 'I'll be waiting for you.'

Then he stood back and let her go.

Kate walked to Rosie's room on very wobbly legs, and when she got there she told Rosie all about where they'd gone. Rosie chattered about her day with Papa Joe, suitably satisfied that she'd missed Saint-Pierre, telling Kate that she'd been there, 'Like, *tons* of times.'

When Kate bent forward to kiss her goodnight, she said, 'Thank you, Rosie, for letting me share your holiday with you and your dad. This is such a special place.'

She was almost at the door when she heard a soft, 'Katie, did your daddy love you?'

Kate stopped dead and turned slowly. She could see Rosie's pale little face in the soft glow of the one lamp. She came back over and sat on the bed. 'What makes you ask that?'

The little girl shrugged. 'My dad—' She stopped and then started again. 'Tiarnan doesn't love me. I'm adopted...he's not even my real dad.'

Kate knew she had to tread carefully. 'Well, sweetie, my dad died a long time ago. I think he loved me—I mean, I'm sure he loved me...even if he didn't really show it.'

Rosie looked at Kate suspiciously. 'What do you mean?'

'Well, he was always very busy. He used to come home late at night, after I'd gone to bed.' She wrinkled her nose. 'And he was worried about work a lot, and money...things like that.'

Rosie looked contemplative for a moment. 'Tiarnan's busy a lot too...but he always tucks me in at night and takes me to school, and if he's away he calls me all the time.' Kate saw her bottom lip quivering. 'But it still doesn't mean he loves me. My mother doesn't love me either...not like Zoe's mum loves her.' A sob broke free and Rosie started crying in earnest, her little shoulders shaking.

Kate gathered Rosie up into her arms and let her cry it out, guessing she'd needed to do this for a long time. She rocked her back and forth, rubbing her back, her heart breaking for the child's pain and confusion.

When the crying had become big hiccupping sighs, Kate pulled back and smoothed Rosie's hair from her flushed face.

She got a tissue from the box nearby and wiped away her tears, made her blow her nose. 'Sweetheart, don't think that. Your dad loves you *so* much.'

'How do you know?' Rosie asked chokily.

Kate tucked some hair behind her ear. 'I know because he always talks about you, and he worries about you and tells everyone about you.' Kate took a bit of poetic licence and mentally crossed her fingers. 'And he's so proud of how well you're settling into your new school. How brave you are to make the change.'

Rosie's face twisted. 'He *made* me change schools and I've no friends now.'

Kate feigned shock. 'What? A stunningly beautiful and funny girl like you? Not possible.' She laid Rosie back against her pillow and then came down close, resting on an arm. 'Do you know? I had to change schools too, when I was just a bit older than you.'

'You did?' Rosie visibly perked up.

Kate nodded. 'And not only that I had to change countries as well. I was living in England, and after my father died my mum moved back to Ireland—right next door to where Auntie Sorcha lived. That's how she and I became best friends. And if I'd never moved country or changed schools I wouldn't have met her...and we wouldn't know each other and I certainly wouldn't know *you,* or be here now.'

'Wow...' Rosie breathed.

'It is hard when things change, but sometimes they change for the better. I bet you're going to have such good friends at the new school. You just have to give it a chance.'

Rosie was plucking at the sheet, looking down. 'Katie, my mummy doesn't want me to go and see her.'

Kate had to hide her visceral reaction. 'Rosie, I'm sure your Mummy loves you...but sometimes adults can be a bit confusing. It's not always easy to understand why they do certain things.' Kate took her hand. 'And you know what? You're lucky to have Tiarnan for a dad, because he loves you twice as much as any other dad.'

'What do you mean?' Rosie looked up with a wary light in her huge brown eyes.

'Even when he found out he wasn't your real dad he made sure to adopt you, so that no one could ever take you away from him. He wanted everyone to know you were his. And I know you still love him, even though you're angry with him.'

Rosie's face got red, and she looked down again.

Kate smoothed her hair. 'It's OK, sweetheart—really it is. Nothing you could do or say will make him stop loving you. He is always going to be there for you, no matter how angry you get, or if he annoys you or if you annoy him, because that's what fathers do.' Kate caught Rosie's eye and made a funny face, tweaking her nose. 'He didn't send you to a horrible nasty cold boarding school in the middle of nowhere, did he?'

Rosie giggled and shook her head. 'No... Katie, tell me a story about you and Auntie Sorcha in school—the one about the midnight feasts.'

Kate kissed her on the forehead and hugged her tight again for a second. 'OK. Just one story and then time for sleep?'

Rosie nodded and gave a big yawn, and by the time Kate was halfway through the first sentence the little girl's eyelids were already drifting shut.

When Kate walked into Tiarnan's room a short while later he lay sleeping on the bed, bare-chested, with the covers riding indecently low on lean hips. Even in sleep he dominated the space around him. She knew she should leave, go to her own bed despite what he'd said, but she felt so full of emotion in that moment she literally couldn't.

She dropped her wrap and went and curled up next to him. Automatically his arm came out and hugged her close to him with a vice-like grip, and Kate knew right then that all her attempts were for naught. Just like that day in the church in France. She could see through her own paltry attempts to protect herself, and she had the awful suspicion that they were failing spectacularly.

A couple of mornings later they were eating breakfast on the wooden terrace. Papa Joe was discussing the garden plants with Tiarnan, Mama Lucille was bustling back and forth, and suddenly Rosie appeared, dragging her bike up the steps from the garden.

'Daddy, can you look at my chain? It's falling off again,' she said.

Kate went completely still, and wondered if Tiarnan had noticed. He and Papa Joe stopped talking. Papa Joe walked away unobtrusively, with an expressive wink at Kate. Kate was about to take the hint and leave too, but Tiarnan shot her a look which told her to stay put.

He went and had a look at the bike and Kate's heart went out to him. He was trying to be so casual. He was fiddling with the bike, but even from here Kate could see the chain looked fine. And then Rosie said, ever so casually, 'Daddy, can we go hiking in the mountains today?'

He looked at Rosie. Kate could see that Rosie was avoiding his eye, scuffing her flip-flop off the ground, as if all this was normal.

Tiarnan's voice was husky. 'I thought you didn't enjoy doing that any more?'

Kate held her breath and to her relief Rosie said, 'I know, but I was thinking I wouldn't mind—and Zoe's in school so I've no one to play with.'

Rosie looked at Kate then and came over, jumping onto her lap to give her a big hug. 'Katie can come too! We can show her all the spiders' nests and things.'

Kate shuddered expressively, and made a face that had Rosie

giggling, 'Yuck! No, thank you very much. I think I can do without seeing where spiders live. I'm not good with creepy-crawly things. You can take pictures.'

Rosie jumped off her lap. 'Silly Katie—it's fun. But it doesn't matter. Me and Daddy can go this time, and you can come next time.'

And with that Rosie hared off into the house, shouting for Mama Lucille to help her pack a picnic for them. Kate's heart had clenched at Rosie's assertion of *next time*.

Tiarnan was standing looking stunned. In shock. He came and sat down and looked at Kate. 'I can't believe it. She hasn't called me Daddy in over a year.'

Kate shrugged. 'Children don't hold grudges for ever.'

He stood again and came around to her seat, hands on either arm of it, trapping her, eyes roving over her face, assessing. 'Why do I have the overwhelming suspicion this has something to do with you? You said goodnight to her for a long time the other night, and she's been unusually quiet these past two days…'

Kate shook her head. Tiarnan's voice had an edge to it that unsettled her. He didn't sound entirely happy with this development. She felt compelled to keep Rosie's counsel, knowing in her heart of hearts that it wouldn't help to divulge how upset she had been.

'We just talked, Tiarnan. She likes hearing stories about me and Sorcha in school. You should go and enjoy the day with your daughter.' Kate forced a smile and tried to shake off the sense of unease that she'd done something wrong. 'I've got a plan to bribe Mama Lucille for some of her secret recipes.'

Despite the fact that he still wasn't smiling, she could sense his relief and sheer happiness. The joy she felt for him scared her, and the realisation hit her like a thunderbolt: she was so deeply in love and bound to Tiarnan Quinn now, and to his daughter, that all she would be able to settle for in her life would be a very pale and insubstantial imitation.

Seeing him just now with Rosie, sensing his innate protectiveness, had rendered any lingering prejudice she might have had about him void. He was nothing like her father. He had a capacity for deep and abiding love, for putting his daughter first. Just no place for a woman or partner in his life… Desolation gripped her like a physical pain.

He spoke then, jerking her out of her reverie, and she was shocked that he didn't seem to see the emotions written all over her face.

'Are you sure you'll be OK here on your own for the day?'

Kate nodded emphatically. Suddenly she wanted nothing more than to be away from the pull of this man's orbit. 'Absolutely.'

Tiarnan seemed to search her eyes, as if looking for something, and then he finally spoke, sounding very stiff and unlike the man who seduced her so ruthlessly every night. 'Very well. We'll be back later—don't wait up; it'll probably be late.'

Kate's sense of unease deepened and lingered right up until the moment she waved Tiarnan and an ecstatic Rosie off in the Jeep.

Late that night Kate found herself waking from a fitful sleep to see the powerful outline of Tiarnan's build as he leant nonchalantly against the doorframe leading out to the balcony, silhouetted by the moonlight. Her first reaction was not of surprise or fear, just immediate joy, and a surge of desire so powerful she shook inside. She sat up.

'Tiarnan…' Her voice was husky from sleep and from that burgeoning desire.

Tiarnan looked at Kate and fought down the intense, nearly overwhelming urge to stop the clamour of voices that mocked him, silence them by going and laying her flat, stripping her bare, taking her so hard and fast that he'd have immediate satisfaction.

Despite the fact that today had proved to be a welcome turning point in his and his daughter's relationship, it had been overshadowed by the bitter realisation that he'd underestimated Kate. He'd put Rosie in an unforgivably vulnerable position. Since the other night, and before Rosie's *volte face* that morning, he'd noticed her introspection, seen how clingy she'd become with Kate, practically overnight. Without looking into it too deeply he'd been thankful that Rosie and Kate got on so well, and had noticed that lack of a central female figure in his daughter's life for the first time in a very concrete way. But that morning everything had been brought into sharp focus, and the time spent away from Kate and her seductive presence had provided the necessary distance for him to see things as they really were.

At first he'd tried to reassure himself that he was being ridiculous. But in his mind's eye all day he'd seen flashes of tender little moments between Rosie and Kate, the easy intimacy that had grown stronger each day, until he couldn't deny the evidence any more—not what it pointed to.

He couldn't *believe* he'd ignored his own instincts and that sensation of vulnerability he'd felt numerous times. He knew with an intense conviction now that Katie had been playing him masterfully all along. From the moment she'd looked at him in France and told him silently of her desire to the feigned reluctance to come with them on holiday and her false concern for Rosie. He'd played into her hands beautifully, all rationality gone in the grip of a lust so powerful he'd been rendered momentarily weak. But not any more.

He'd given her an opportunity and she'd adroitly taken every chance to inveigle her way in. He had no one to blame but himself. She'd admitted only the other night that she had no intention of settling down any time soon, and yet she'd obviously seen a way to assure herself a strong position as his mistress by using Rosie. And it was entirely his fault. He simply could not see another reason for her behaviour. His own mother and Stella had both proved to be woefully inept mother figures—

how could someone like Kate, an international model, possibly be any different? Especially with a child who wasn't even her own? Self-recrimination burned him deep inside.

Kate watched as Tiarnan straightened from the door and walked towards her slowly. Tension and that sense of unease was back with a vengeance. He stopped at the foot of the bed, his legs in a wide, unmistakably dominant stance. Arms folded. None of the teasing, lazily smiling seductiveness he usually displayed.

'We're leaving tomorrow.'

His words fell like shards of glass. Kate was completely nonplussed, had no clue as to what he was talking about or why it felt like a slap in the face.

'But…I thought we had at least another four days here? Has something happened?'

He shook his head, and then laughed harshly. 'You could say that. I've realised that I made a grave error of judgement in bringing you here.'

Pain lanced Kate, and she felt unbelievably vulnerable in her plain T-shirt, her head still a little fuzzy from sleep. 'What do you mean?'

Tiarnan came around, closer to the bed. Kate fought not to shrink back and looked up. The blue of his eyes was intense despite the dim light.

'I shouldn't have trusted that you wouldn't use Rosie in some kind of manipulative effort to gain a more intimate place in our lives—my life. A more permanent position. I can see now that that's *exactly* what you were doing in your own quiet little way.'

Suddenly Kate was wide awake. Without really thinking she sprang out of the bed to stand beside it, her heart hammering. 'What on earth are you talking about?' She shook because she was in such shock, so affronted. 'I would *never* use Rosie like that. How could you think such a thing?'

Tiarnan's face was harsher than she'd ever seen it. 'Because you said something to her the other night and she's now developed a sense of devotion to you that you've undoubtedly engineered for your own ends.'

Tiarnan thought again of the day he'd just spent with his daughter—her easy chatter about everything and anything that he'd missed so much, and how it had been interspersed with countless references to Katie this and Katie that. He'd had no idea that Kate had insinuated herself so subtly into their lives—and more importantly into Rosie's life. The child clearly had a case of hero-worship—no doubt fostered by Kate herself.

Kate drew herself up to her full height, unbelievably hurt that Tiarnan could think such a thing. And yet she knew she couldn't, *wouldn't* betray Rosie's confidence.

'I'm very fond of Rosie, and I'm flattered that she likes me. She's a very lovable little girl. But I would never foster intimacy with her just to get some kind of closer relationship with you, as you're suggesting.'

Tiarnan unfolded his arms and made a slashing gesture that forced Kate to take a step back. She'd never seen him look so angry, and realised that it was an intense anger at himself. Her heart ached in the face of his blatant mistrust, that he could believe that he had put Rosie in any kind of danger.

'There's a good reason I've never invited a woman into my life on such an intimate level. For you I made an exception, because we have a shared history and because you're not a stranger to Rosie. But it was a grave error, and it's one I'm going to rectify immediately—before Rosie can grow any more attached to you. I take full responsibility. I should never have allowed you to look after her in Madrid in the first place, or invited you here.' *Why had he thought for a second that she would be any different from any other woman?*

Kate folded her arms, willing the hurt from her voice. 'So you're going to banish me from your sight and from Rosie's presence? What about Rosie? What is *she* going to think if I suddenly disappear?'

He came close and put a finger under her chin to tip her face up. Kate clenched her jaw, refusing to let him see how badly he was affecting her.

'I've told Rosie that you've been called home for work. You can say goodbye to her in the morning. I'll escort you back to Madrid. I have some urgent business to attend to there for a couple of days, and then I'll return here alone to spend the rest of the holiday with Rosie.'

Anger rushed through Kate at his high-handed manner and she bit out, 'You don't have to escort me anywhere, Tiarnan. I'm not going to steal the silver on my way out. Need I remind you that I never wanted to come here in the first place?'

Tiarnan quirked his brow. His voice was like steel, reminding her of how intent he'd been on seducing her that night in San Francisco. It grated across Kate's nerves.

'I'll escort you because, as I said, I've business to attend to. And need I remind *you* that it took just one night to act out your charade of playing hard to get before you agreed to come here?'

Shame coursed through Kate. He was right. But it had been no charade.

Before she knew what was happening Tiarnan was pulling her close, reaching for the hem of her T-shirt to pull it up. Kate slapped his hands away ineffectually, incensed that he would think he could speak to her like this, accuse her of this, and still seduce her.

'What do you think you're doing?'

'I'm taking you to bed—which is what I should have remembered is the primary focus of this relationship.'

Kate pulled back within the tight band of steel of his arms, trying desperately to avoid his head as it lowered, his mouth intoxicatingly close to hers. She shook her head from side to side, felt Tiarnan catch a long skein of her hair, holding her head still.

'*No!* I won't do this. I don't deserve this, Tiarnan. It was your decision to ask me here. I did not manipulate you in any way. And I did *not* take advantage of Rosie.'

Her words sliced into Tiarnan with the precision of a knife, reminding him of his misjudgement once again. He drew back, but held her close. Angled his hips and moved them against hers so that she could feel his arousal. He saw the flare of helpless response in her eyes, saw it race across her cheeks in a blaze of colour. Triumph surged through him. He felt as if he was back in control.

'Well, then—if, as you say, you've no intention of using Rosie, and never wanted to be here in the first place, you can't possibly object to going home, can you?'

Kate stilled in her struggle, and felt an empty ache spread outwards from her heart. She might not have wanted to come here initially—but she had, and she'd seen a slice of paradise that had more to do with the family idyll she'd always craved and less to do with the stunning surroundings. But of course Tiarnan could never know that. So she hitched her chin and said, coolly and clearly, 'No. I couldn't think of anything I'd like more than to go home.'

'Good.' Tiarnan's voice was grim, and rough with barely leashed desire.

Kate heard it and her treacherous body responded. She knew at that moment that this was it. Once they returned to Madrid the next day she was going to walk away from Tiarnan and move on with her life.

So now, when he pulled her closer and his mouth found hers, she emitted a growl of angry, hurt capitulation, but she allowed him to sweep her along in the tide of desire that blew up around them because it would be for the last time.

CHAPTER EIGHT

THE journey back to Madrid was uneventful. Kate looked out of the window and saw that they were approaching landing. Relief should have flooded her, but it didn't—only heaviness. Tiarnan was immersed in paperwork and Kate was glad of the reprieve. She'd been terrified that he'd attempt to seduce her on the plane and that she wouldn't be able to hold her emotions back. She'd barely managed to hold them back last night after they'd made love and, despite the tension tinged with anger on both sides, Tiarnan had brought her to a point of such transcendence that she'd cried silent tears afterwards. He hadn't seen, though, and she'd feigned sleep, waiting for and willing him to return to his own bed, which he eventually had done, leaving her mortifyingly bereft.

The plane landed and the stewards escorted them out. Kate spied the car she'd ordered from Martinique waiting in the distance, and finally the relief she craved flooded her. Tiarnan's own car was pulled up by the steps. He gestured for her to give the driver her bag but she clung onto it. He frowned at her, a man clearly not patient with being made to wait for anything. He held out his hand.

'Your bag, Kate.'

Kate shook her head and backed away, looked over her shoulder to the other car. 'That's my car there, Tiarnan. I'm booked on a flight back to New York from here, I don't have much time.'

His eyes speared her and she quivered inwardly.

'Don't be ridiculous. You can stay with me until I have to return to Martinique.'

Kate smiled, and it felt brittle and false. 'Is that what you see happening? Now that I'm safely out of Rosie's way we can continue this affair until such time as you or I get bored?'

Tiarnan frowned even more deeply, an uncomfortable prickling sensation running over his skin. He wasn't used to women articulating his inner thoughts. That was exactly how he'd envisaged things going. He'd removed what he'd seen as a threat to Rosie from her life, which allowed him to continue his affair with Kate. He made a discreet gesture and knew that his driver had melted away into the car behind him.

He gestured with his hand again, and didn't like the sense of desperation gripping his innards. 'Come on, Kate. Let's not waste time.'

She shook her head again, more emphatically. 'No. I told you before this affair was only going to last for the holiday, and it's over now.' She forced the words out, even though they were like broken glass lacerating her tongue. 'Thank you for taking me. I had a nice time.'

A nice time? Tiarnan felt so incandescent his vision was blurred for a moment. He had the strongest, most primal urge to pick Kate up, throw her in the back of his car and instruct Juan to drive and keep driving until his head was clear of this gnarled heat.

'Kate, you don't have to act out this charade. I want you. But I'm not going to play games pursuing you all over the world. I'm quite happy for you to be my mistress. I just won't have you use Rosie as a pawn to get there.'

The pain was intense, but Kate forced herself to stay standing. 'I'm not playing games, Tiarnan. I don't do that. I meant what I said. This is over.'

The quiet intensity of her voice suddenly told him that she spoke the truth. And in that instant unwelcome and burning came the suspicion that he'd grossly misjudged her motives where Rosie was concerned. He couldn't deny that he'd acted out of a knee-jerk sense of panic that he'd done something wrong—that he'd allowed someone into their intimate sphere who could harm Rosie exactly as Stella had. The truth was, he'd simply never seen Rosie trust a woman so implicitly who wasn't either Sorcha, her grandmother, or Mama Lucille and her family…

Kate stood in front of him and she'd never looked lovelier. Her flawless skin had taken on a warm honey glow, and her hair had streaks of platinum among the blonde strands. She was dressed in a simple white shirt and jeans, and he noticed the straw hat she held in one clenched hand. It was the tacky hat he'd bought her in Saint-Pierre. Suddenly a memory hit him right between the eyes: the evening they'd returned from that outing she'd caught him about to throw it away, with the sunglasses. She'd grabbed them from him with surprising force and said, 'Don't!'

And then jokingly, as if to diminish it, 'I plan on showing them to one of my designer friends. You never know—they could inspire his next collection.'

But it was her eyes that had caught him. They hadn't been joking. They'd been deadly serious.

Right then, standing by his car, a lot of things seemed to be clicking into place. Everything that had happened between them seemed to merge into one memory, and he recalled how she'd looked at him when he'd pulled back from their kiss ten years ago—the light that had shone out of her just before he'd asked her what the hell she was thinking. He could see now that he'd forgotten how that light had dimmed…but the memory of her vulnerability was suddenly vivid.

He backed away, the compulsion to drag her off by her hair

curiously fading. And yet he felt empty inside. Twisted with conflicting emotions.

'Yes,' he said, not even sure what he was replying to. 'Thanks for coming with us, Kate, I'm sure I'll see you soon.'

Kate paled and she looked uncertain—as if she'd expected more of a fight, as if she were almost disappointed. 'Yes. No doubt. And, Tiarnan?'

He stopped and looked at her, feeling numb.

'Please don't feel that you have to give me anything…like a token… If you do, I'll just send it back.'

And then she turned and walked away quickly, that hat in one hand, her case in the other. Tiarnan watched as a driver leapt out of the other car and took her case, then waited till she sat inside and closed the door behind her. Then the car was pulling away and she was gone.

Two weeks later. The Ritz Hotel, Central Park, New York

'I'm afraid I'm not a very good dancer, William.'

Kate forced a smile at the man whose arm was far too tight around her waist as he led her to the dance floor through the throng. He was her date for the evening and, as for how getting on with her life was going, things were pretty dismal.

He breathed in her ear—far too close for her liking, 'I don't believe it for a second. It's impossible you can't dance well.'

Kate mentally told him, *You've been warned.* She'd been invited to this glitzy charity function by the honourable William Fortwin the Third, the pampered son of a well-known media mogul. And she'd come because she had to at least give him a chance. Now she wished she was anywhere but here. Her feet ached from working all day and her dress was too tight. She put it down to Mama Lucille's cooking, and then abruptly diverted her mind from that dangerous avenue of thought.

Her breasts felt almost unbearably sensitive too—and, come

to think of it, she felt sensitive all over, and bloated. It had to be down to her overdue period… She was practically bursting out of her dress, which wasn't a good thing as it was strapless and had a provocative slit to the thigh. She really didn't need William to have any more encouragement to look at her cleavage.

She sighed deeply as he swung her a little too enthusiastically onto the dance floor, and resolutely moved his hand back up to her waist from her bottom—*again*.

Tiarnan watched Kate move the man's hand from her bottom and unclenched his own hands a little. But everything else stayed clenched. He hadn't expected to see her here tonight; how many functions had he been to in New York over the years and never bumped into her?

And yet ever since he'd touched down in New York she'd filled his mind so completely that at first he'd thought he was hallucinating when he'd seen her. All thoughts of the business deal he was meant to be wrapping up were gone. And he had to concede now that she'd been filling his mind constantly in the last two weeks. Returning to Martinique and Rosie should have been a balm to his spirit. But it had proved to be anything but. It had seemed lacklustre, empty. Even his improved relationship with Rosie had failed to lift his spirits, and at every turn people had seemed to mention Kate and ask about her, ask when she might come back. She'd created an indelible impression in just a few days.

That sense that he'd misjudged her had been compounded even more so when Rosie had finally revealed what she and Kate had talked about that night. He could see now that Rosie had needed that outlet desperately—someone independent that she could confide in, someone who wasn't him. And from what he could gather Kate had reassured her with a gentle intuition that had done anything *but* take advantage of the vulnerable little girl.

He took her in. She looked stunning. Her dress was a champagne colour, and her skin glowed with the remnants of her tan even from where he stood. Her hair was swept up and kept in place with a diamanté pin, baring her neck, which made Tiarnan feel inordinately protective. There was something about her tonight that he hadn't noticed before—a kind of *glow*. She was undeniably beautiful, but it seemed to be radiating right out of her in a way he'd never seen before.

The crowd cleared for a moment, and Tiarnan saw the man's hand descend to Kate's bottom again—just as the thigh-high slit in her dress revealed one long shapely leg. It was too much. Restraining himself from physically throwing people aside, he went out to the lobby, where he spoke briefly to the receptionist and then went back into the ballroom.

As he walked towards her now, with one goal in mind, all the nebulous tendrils of revelation and doubt he'd felt that evening standing before her at Madrid airport were conveniently forgotten in the mist of this lust haze clouding his vision. Also forgotten was the fact that he'd felt that instinctive need to let her walk away. He couldn't fathom right now how on earth he'd let her go.

Kate felt a prickling on her neck, and as she apologised to William for what seemed like the umpteenth time she wondered if perhaps she was coming down with flu. Then she heard a deep drawling voice behind her, and would have fallen if not for the fact that she was being held in such a grip.

'She really is a terrible dancer—I'm sure you won't mind if I cut in.'

It wasn't a question, it was a thinly veiled threat, an imperative, and William Fortwin recognised a superior male when he saw one. He dropped Kate like a hot coal, much to her chagrin and relief.

'Of course. Here…'

And before she knew what was happening Tiarnan Quinn had smoothly inserted himself into William's place. Suddenly

Kate's evening exploded into a million tiny balls of sensation. Her head felt light, she no longer felt constricted…or she did, but it was a different kind of constriction. Shock rendered her momentarily speechless. Lust and heat were intense and immediate after a two-week absence. All efforts to forget about this man and his effect on her were shown up in all their pathetic ineffectiveness.

And with that shaming realisation, as if she hadn't done the hardest thing she'd ever done in her life just walking away from him two weeks ago, she allowed anger to rise. She would *never* forget the way he'd so grossly misjudged her, letting his innate cynicism distort her innocent friendship with Rosie. Or the way he'd let her walk away from him in Madrid and, even more shamingly, the way that despite all her precious efforts to self-protect she'd longed for him to haul her back to him and demand she stay. He'd morphed in an instant that evening from hot and astounded to cool and distant, and she'd been terrified that he'd seen something of her real feelings. Her eyes flashed what she hoped were real sparks.

'What do you think you're doing?' she spat. 'That man was my date.' This was punctuated with an accidental stepping on Tiarnan's toes. He didn't even wince.

'You need to dance with someone who can handle your lack of…shall we say…skill?' He quirked his beautiful mouth.

Kate saw red at his easy seductive insouciance. 'You can't just order him off like a dog.'

Tiarnan's mouth thinned. 'I just did. That man wasn't fit to clean your shoes and you know it. You would have put up with the dance, feigned a headache and insisted you had to go home alone.'

Kate gasped, aghast. It was exactly what she'd been planning on doing. She coloured, and Tiarnan looked triumphant.

She smiled sweetly. 'Well, then, you can save me the bother of saying the same to you.'

He didn't respond, just seemed to be transfixed by her mouth—which made her groin tingle and her breasts tighten even more painfully. She began to feel desperate. He had to go.

'*What* are you doing here? Or did you somehow manipulate it so that I'd be asked here on a date just so you could cut in?'

He didn't look in the least bit insulted, and Kate tried valiantly not to notice how stupendously gorgeous he was in his tuxedo, even darker and more dangerous-looking after the holiday.

'I'm here on business. But the business side of things paled into insignificance the minute I saw you across the room.'

The uncomfortable realisation struck him that the business side of things had paled into insignificance long before tonight.

Kate stood on his feet again, but he merely whirled her further into the dance floor. She had to acknowledge that along with a sense of exasperation that he was here was also—much more treacherously—an intense joy she couldn't deny. To be in his arms again was such heaven, and even more so when contrasted with her hapless date.

Kate struggled not to let her eyes close as she repeated in her head like a mantra: *Just get through the dance…just get through the dance.* She had the awful feeling she wouldn't have the strength to walk away from him again, even if he was cool and distant. A humiliating image rose in her mind of her clinging onto his feet like a whipped puppy.

And then he bent his head low and whispered with bone tingling intimacy, 'I want you, Kate. You've kept me awake for two weeks.'

Kate jerked back and looked up, her eyes growing wide. She was shaking all over—and inside. She felt so torn that she was close to tears, unbelievably raw at seeing him here like this, taken by surprise. As if sensing weakness, Tiarnan kissed the edge of her mouth fleetingly, his tongue making the merest dart of sensation against her lips. It was enough to set off a chain reaction of desire throughout her body so strong that she could only look at him helplessly and follow him, her hand in his, as he strode off the dance floor and through the crowd. Desire transcended everything, and it eclipsed Kate's need to self-protect.

He didn't hesitate or deviate for a second, as if knowing how close Kate was to turning tail and running. They got into the lift, neither one looking at the other, just at the numbers as they ascended. Kate's hand was still in a tight grip with Tiarnan's much larger one.

The lift came to a smooth halt and the doors opened with silent luxuriousness. Tiarnan led them into a plush corridor and took out a room key to open a door. Kate vaguely took in the sumptuous room, with its grand view over the darkened outlines of Central Park lit up by moonlight in a clear sky. The lights of the city glittered and twinkled.

But she didn't care about views or luxurious rooms or any of that. She only cared about Tiarnan, and the fact that he had to touch her now or she'd die. As if reading her mind he threw off his jacket with an almost violent movement—and then she was in his arms and his mouth was on hers. And it felt so right. So good. So necessary.

They were still standing. Kate kicked off her shoes. She felt Tiarnan snake a hand up under all the chiffon folds of her dress. She gasped against his mouth when he reached her pants. He pulled them down; she kicked them off, urgency making her clumsy.

She struggled with and finally tore off his bow tie, opened his shirt to bare his chest, reached down between them to open his belt and release him. All the while their mouths were fused, as if it was too much to break apart even for a second.

Kate felt the clip being pulled from her hair, and the heavy mass fell down around her shoulders. Tiarnan's hand luxuriated in the strands, massaging her head in an incongruously tender gesture amidst the passionate urgency.

She finally managed to pull down his trousers, freeing his

heavy erection. His hands were under her dress, lifting it up. Kate raised her leg and cried out when she felt Tiarnan lift her against the door and thrust up into her in one smooth move.

For a moment, as if savouring the intensity, neither one moved or breathed, and then, because it was too exquisite not to, they moved. Kate wrapped her arms around his neck and clenched her buttocks. Tiarnan let out a long hiss of breath. They moved in tandem, surrounded by nothing but their breathing and their frantic heartbeats as Tiarnan drove in and out, taking them higher and higher, his chest heaving against Kate's which felt unbearably swollen against her dress.

When the pinnacle came, it seemed to go on for ever. Tiarnan had to soothe Kate, tell her it was OK to let go, before she finally allowed herself to fall, let the release sweep her away. Tiarnan joined her, and when they were finally spent he buried his head in her neck. It had been fast and furious. Shattering.

After what seemed like ages, Tiarnan finally let Kate down. Her legs were unbelievably wobbly. She muttered something and went to find the bathroom, locking herself inside with relief while she tried to gather her wits and come to terms with what she'd just let happen.

Her mind was barely able to function, but uppermost was a need to protect and survive. She had to get away from Tiarnan. After a few minutes she stood and looked in the mirror. She was wearing more make-up than she normally would and was glad of it now. Somehow she'd had the wherewithal to pick up her pants and hair clip. With shaking hands she stepped back into her underwear and pinned her hair back up—a little untidily, but it would have to do. And then, taking a deep breath, she went back out to the suite.

She came out to see Tiarnan smile at her with sexy laziness, in the act of taking off his cufflinks. His trousers were open at the top, shirt undone. All her good intentions nearly flew out of the window. *Nearly*.

She called on the cool reserve that felt so alien and hard to muster now and said, 'I meant what I said in Madrid, Tiarnan. It's over. And that—' she looked accusingly at the door '—shouldn't have happened.'

'Well, it did,' he drawled, and indicated to the bed. 'I've got the suite for the night.'

Kate looked at the bed. She was angry, because a very big part of her was tempted to just give in, throw caution to the wind and indulge in another ten hours of bliss. But then when and where would it stop? She had to be strong—had to do this now once and for all.

She shook her head and stood her ground. 'No, Tiarnan. I'm not staying the night. Much as I might be tempted, it's not going to happen.'

He stopped what he was doing and looked at her. She didn't look as if she wanted to hang around. Irritation and frustration prickled under his skin. He wanted her already again. Painfully. Urgently. The frustration of the past two weeks still shocked him with its intensity.

He couldn't stop the impatience lacing his voice. He was a man used to getting what he wanted, when he wanted. 'Look, Kate, you want me—I want you. We're good together. What's the problem?'

Kate wanted to scream; was it always this simple for men? She answered herself: it was if they didn't have feelings invested. Tiarnan started to walk towards her and panic made her jerky. She flung out a hand. 'Stop! Don't come any closer.' She knew if he so much as touched her she'd be a mess.

He stopped and frowned.

'Whatever we are is neither here nor there, Tiarnan. I'm not in the market for an affair. I just won't do it.'

'Well, I wouldn't call what we're doing an *affair*—we know each other, we're friends…it's more than that.'

He didn't even trust her with his daughter. Sadness and pain gripped Kate. 'It's *not* more than that because you don't trust me, Tiarnan. But that's beside the point—because it's going to come to an end, isn't it?'

Tiarnan wasn't sure where this was going. 'Well, of course it will—at some stage. But does it have to be tonight? Right now?'

Kate nodded and held back a sob. 'I can't do this. With you.'

She started walking to the door. Before she got to it Tiarnan reached her and turned her around.

She looked up, stiff all over, feeling more constricted than ever. 'Please, Tiarnan—just let me go.'

A muscle clenched in his jaw. She could see the confusion in his eyes. And then he said, 'Tell me why—just tell me why you don't want to do this.'

She looked at him for a long moment and knew that there was only one way he would let her walk away. She would have to bare her soul. Even so, she asked, 'Do you really want to know?'

He nodded. Grim. Determined.

She pushed past him back into the room, putting space between them. She paced for a minute, and then stopped and looked at him, summoned all her courage. 'Because that night ten years ago took way more out of me than I revealed to you at the time.'

He frowned, his black brows creasing over those stunning blue eyes.

Kate continued, but every word was costing her an emotional lifetime. 'That night…I'd no intention of trying to seduce you. I…' She faltered and looked away, then back again. 'I'd had a crush on you for a long time, Tiarnan, and that night I thought I saw you notice me as a woman for the first time. I somehow got the courage to kiss you…and you kissed me back…'

'So…?'

Kate could see he was trying to figure it out. 'I guessed you believed I was more confident that I really was. But then, when you rejected me, I wanted to protect myself—pretend that I'd been in full control. I felt humiliated, and I hated that you might see how much it had meant to me.'

Tiarnan had the strangest sensation of the earth shifting beneath his feet, but he stayed standing. He'd had that instinct, but then when she'd seemed to sure…so mature…so cool… he'd doubted it. But he shouldn't have. It was the vulnerability he'd sensed in Martinique. And at the airport in Madrid, when it had compelled him to let her walk away.

He tried to cling onto something. 'What does that have to do with *now?*'

'Everything!' Kate wailed, throwing up her arms, taking him by surprise.

Colour was high in her cheeks. Her eyes sparkled like jewels and he felt a chasm opening up between them.

Her chest rose and fell with agitation. 'I've been aware of you for the past ten years, Tiarnan. Every time I've looked at you I've remembered that kiss. The pitifully few and far between men I've been with have all come a far distant second to the way I imagined *you* might have made me feel.' Her voice cracked ominously. 'How pathetic is that? They fell short of little more than my imagination. I couldn't even form a decent lasting relationship because the shadow you'd cast made everyone else pale in comparison.'

Her mouth twisted bitterly, making Tiarnan want to kiss the bitter line away, hating that he had caused it.

'Over the years I learnt to protect myself. I never wanted you to know how I'd failed to get over you. But at the christening that day it was so hard to stand there and witness Sorcha and Romain's joy and love with you right beside me…and then in San Francisco…I couldn't hide it any more.'

She shrugged again, and it made something lance Tiarnan's heart, but he couldn't move.

'I agreed to go to Martinique with you because I thought it might help…that by sleeping with you it might somehow make you fall off your pedestal. Reduce what we had shared to something more banal. But it didn't, Tiarnan. It's made things worse. I can't do this. And I would never have used Rosie in any kind of manipulative way. I *hate* that you would think that.' She shook her head and made for the door again.

Feeling panic surge, Tiarnan gripped her shoulders and pulled her around, tipping her chin up. Her eyes were closed. He grabbed her hands and brought them up, holding them tightly, manacled in his. 'Kate—look at me.'

She shook her head, and he could see her press her lips together in a desperate attempt at control. A tear trickled out from under the long lashes that rested on her flushed cheek. He felt weak inside. Utterly helpless. And like the biggest heel.

'Kate—please, don't cry. I owe you a huge apology. I'm sorry for accusing you of using Rosie. I can see how wrong I was.'

The full extent of his own cynicism hit him forcibly. It was so clear now. He'd lashed out as much in an effort to protect himself as Rosie, and the realisation disgusted him. Kate had just got too close too quickly. She opened her eyes then, and the naked emotion in their swimming depths put him to shame. But he couldn't let go of her wrists. He felt the frantic beat of her pulse and it reminded him of a caged bird.

In a hoarse voice filled with emotion she said, 'This is who I really am, Tiarnan, and what I really want: if I never had to stand in front of a photographer again to have my photo taken or parade down a catwalk I'd be ecstatic. My idea of a good Saturday night is staying in and baking bread. I like knitting— and I like to crochet if I'm really going out on a limb. I make homemade soup. What I want more than anything in the world is to find someone to love who'll love me back and to have babies with them—lots of babies—and raise a family. That's what I want and need. I've no idea if that's as a result of my emotionally barren childhood or conditioning or whatever. All I know is that it's what I want in the deepest core part of me.

I'm not the kind of person who can have an affair and not get involved. And I would never ask any of this from you because I know you've done it. You've got it. You're happy. But I'm not, Tiarnan, and as much as we might have *this*...' she jerked her head to the bed '...it's not enough for me.'

She pulled her hands to try and free them, but he held on with something like a death grip.

'*Please* let me go, so I can get over you and get on with my life.'

Tiarnan stood in silence, stunned to his very depths. Shocked. In awe of this passionate Kate—a different kind of passionate that he'd never seen before. A huge block prevented him from speaking. She was looking up at him defiantly, as if daring him to seduce her again, knowing everything he now knew. She'd give in if he just kissed her. He knew she'd give in. They both knew. It permeated the air around them. But how could he do that?

The revelations he'd acknowledged when he realised that she *hadn't* been a dim and distant memory for him throughout the past ten years seemed so pathetic now, compared to her feelings. He knew he couldn't even begin to articulate that without sounding as if he was making excuses. It would be like trying to placate her—or, worse, patronise her.

She looked so young at that moment, so beautiful. His instinct had been right that day at the airport when he'd seen her holding onto that ridiculous hat. He'd seen something momentarily unguarded in her eyes. He realised now that it had been her attempt to make the break.

She was right. She deserved her happiness. She deserved to find a good man who would love her the way she wanted to be loved and give her all the babies and joy she wanted. Something in him reacted forcibly to that image but he forced it down. He had no right to it. No right to feel jealous.

All of a sudden he felt tired and jaded and cynical. He'd been there and had been badly burned in the process. He had always vowed never to expose himself like that again. He had Rosie. He had Sorcha and her family. Kate deserved more. He had to let her go.

Kate dropped her head. She couldn't keep looking Tiarnan in the eye, seeing the myriad emotions as he finally came to the realisation, as she knew he would, that he wouldn't be able to get rid of her fast enough. She sensed it before it even happened. He dropped her hands from his grip and stepped back. He was letting her go again. And this time she knew it was for good.

She couldn't look up. 'Thank you,' she said faintly.

His deep voice impacted like a punch in her solar plexus. 'You deserve to find what you want, Kate. I wish you all the best.'

A couple of days later Tiarnan stood in his office in Madrid, staring out of the window with his hands in his pockets. The fact that he *never* stood staring vacantly out of the window was not something that impinged on his consciousness. His eminently professional assistant knocked on his door and came in. He didn't notice the fleeting look of alarm cross her face just before he turned to face her. 'Maria?'

She came towards him and held out a brown padded envelope. 'This came for you just after you'd left for New York. It's marked "Private". I didn't want to open it.'

Tiarnan took it and had a strange feeling. He dismissed Maria and turned the envelope over. On the back, in the same clear, neat writing as on the front, was a familiar New York address and the name K. Lancaster.

He sat at his desk and opened it. Out fell a sheaf of glossy black and white photos. With his hands none too steady he looked through them, becoming more and more amazed and seriously impressed. They were stunning, and all taken completely off guard: pictures of him with Rosie, pictures of Mama

Lucille and Papa Joe, moments snatched. And he hadn't even been aware of her taking the pictures.

There was another smaller envelope, marked for Rosie. Tiarnan couldn't help himself. He had to open it. So far there were no pictures of Kate. The photo that fell out was of Kate and Rosie making funny faces at the camera, which must have been on a timer. And on the back was a note.

Rosie, I miss you already. Please know that I'd love you to come and visit me any time, and the next time I'm in Madrid we'll go out for ice cream—I'll be looking forward to hearing all about your new friends. In the meantime take care. Love, Katie.

It was only after a long moment that he realised he'd been holding his breath. He carefully put the photo back into the envelope. He stood up abruptly and went again to the window.

He couldn't want her this badly—so badly that a photograph of her pulling a funny face made him feel weak. Grim determination settled around him like a weight. She was gone. He had to let her be. She was right. He had his life. He had Rosie. He didn't need anything else, didn't want anything else. Maybe if he kept repeating it he'd start to believe it.

CHAPTER NINE

Six weeks later. Madison Avenue, New York.

KATE huddled deeper into her long padded coat and wrapped her scarf tighter around her neck. It was coming up to Christmas, and the shops were alive and bright with decorations and lights. They twinkled merrily in the dusk. She felt removed from it all, though—she was in total shock. She'd just come from an evening clinic with her doctor. Her awful growing suspicion of the last few weeks was now confirmed. There was a reason the bloated feeling had never gone away, and a reason for the fact that her breasts were so sensitive it hurt to touch them. And a very good reason for the fact that she hadn't had her period yet.

She was pregnant.

Over two months pregnant.

She stumbled on the sidewalk and someone automatically put out a hand to steady her, Kate smiled her thanks and kept going. But she felt as though everything was starting to disintegrate around her. She had to get home. She unconsciously started walking faster, sudden tears blurring her vision, and looked down to avoid people's eyes. Right in that moment she'd never felt so alone in all her life.

On the one hand, despite the shock, she felt the pure ecstatic joy of being pregnant, and on the other hand she felt the sheer desolation of knowing that the father would only see this as a burden or, worse, as something planned to trap him in some way. How could he not when it had happened before?

Why, oh why, had she blurted everything out to Tiarnan that night? Kate had remonstrated bitterly with herself ever since. The only thing she could give any thanks for was the fact that she hadn't come straight out and told him that she loved him.

But, she reminded herself, she hadn't needed to. She'd all but prostrated herself at his feet.

Kate unseeingly followed the mass of humans who were walking down Madison Avenue, her mind and belly churning sickly. All of a sudden, out of nowhere, she hit a brick wall. But it was a brick wall with hands and arms, steadying her. God, she couldn't even manage to walk down the street without avoiding mishap.

She looked up to apologise and her world stopped turning. She had the absurd impulse to laugh for a hysterical moment, before cold, stark reality set in.

'No,' she breathed painfully. 'It can't be you.'

'Kate? Is that you?'

It *was* Tiarnan. Looking down at her with dark brows pulled over piercing blue eyes. In a dark coat. Kate cursed fate and the gods, and at the same time had an awful soul-destroying awareness of how impossibly handsome he looked. How was it that she'd managed beautifully for ten years to avoid him and suddenly he seemed to be around every corner? And yet even amongst the shock and despair of seeing him she couldn't control her body's response, the awful kick of her heart.

'Yes, it's me. Sorry, I wasn't looking where I was going.' She attempted to be civil, normal, and completely and conveniently blocked out the fact that she'd just found out that she was pregnant and that the father stood in front of her right now. An extreme urge to self-protect was strong. 'How are you, Tiarnan?'

He was still holding her, looking at her strangely. Almost absently, he answered, 'Fine. Fine...'

It was only at that moment that Kate noticed someone hovering behind him. A woman. A petite, very beautiful, very soignée brunette, who smiled icily at Kate. It was all the impetus she needed. She was raw with the news she'd just received. Too raw to cope with this.

She stepped away, dislodging Tiarnan's hands, and noticed for the first time where they were. Kate had bumped into Tiarnan as he'd been walking into a restaurant. The same exclusive restaurant outside which she'd bumped into him dressed as a French maid some years before. With another dark-haired beauty. He'd obviously reverted to type.

Before she could lose it completely there on the path, in front of the man she loved and his lover, she fled. Exactly as she'd done before. Except this time Tiarnan had seen her and recognised her. The humiliation was so much worse this time, and the awful irony of coming full circle was nearly too much to bear.

Tiarnan watched as Kate strode away, her bright hair like a beacon among the sea of anonymous people. He still felt the force of her body slamming into him, full-on. He still saw her upturned face, those huge eyes. She'd looked pale—too pale. And tired. Concern clutched him. And a sudden feeling of *déjà vu*.

'Tiarnan? Are we going in? And who was that woman? She looked incredibly familiar.'

Tiarnan finally noticed his date again for the first time. He'd only asked her out in some kind of pathetic attempt to regain something close to normal in his life, but he knew now that he'd just watched his only hope of being normal again walk away. When he'd held Kate steady for those brief moments just now he'd felt at peace for the first time in weeks. A deep sigh of relief had moved through him.

He tried to focus on his date. 'Melinda, I'm sorry, but something's come up. I'm going to have to cancel dinner.'

He was already urging her back to his car at the kerb. He heard a very piqued, 'It's *Miranda,* actually—'

He opened the car door and ushered the woman in with little finesse, saying to his driver, 'Please take Miranda—sorry, Melinda—wherever she wants to go.'

Tiarnan slammed the door and watched the car pull away with an inordinate sense of relief. He started walking in the opposite direction to the one Kate had taken; as much as he wanted nothing more than to go to her straight away, he knew he had to handle this carefully. Impatience and urgency coursed through him, but for once in his life he had to control it. He had some serious thinking to do.

Kate felt as washed out as a dishrag. It was as if hearing from the doctor that she was pregnant had kick-started her body to react, and morning sickness had arrived with a vengeance. She finally emerged from the bathroom with her hand on her belly, which was feeling hard and surprisingly big already, now that she knew she wasn't just bloated. But she knew why that was. Her mind just shied away from thinking too much about it at the moment.

She was finding it hard to process everything, and also the fact that she'd bumped into Tiarnan last night. The pain of seeing him with that woman was buried deep. She still couldn't even begin to think about how she was going to tell him…and Sorcha… A welcome numbness came over her and she knew it was some kind of protective barrier, stopping the pain and hurt from impinging too deeply. She gave up silent thanks that she didn't have to work today, and then her head hurt at the thought of breaking the news to Maud too that she was pregnant. Her lingerie contract would be out of the window— not that Kate would be sorry.

A knock came on her door, and Kate started. She couldn't deny the fact that after seeing Tiarnan in the street she'd half expected him to turn up at her door behind her. And when he hadn't…the shame of how much she'd wanted it and the pain that he hadn't had been indescribable. She reassured herself now that it could only be someone from inside the building, as the concierge usually rang up if there was a visitor. It was probably the super—or Mrs Goldstein from next door.

As she approached the door she pulled a cardigan from the chair by the door and put it on. She was only dressed in ancient sweatpants and an old T-shirt of Sorcha's.

She opened the door, and when she took in who was on the other side she could feel the colour drain from her face. Her hand tightened on the knob. She instinctively clutched the cardigan around her belly, ridiculously glad she'd had the fore-sight to put it on.

'Tiarnan.'

'Kate.'

For an absurd moment neither spoke. They just looked at one another. Kate heard Mrs Goldstein's door creak open, and a voice with a thick New York accent asked, 'Kate? Are you OK?'

Kate dragged her gaze from Tiarnan's and stuck her head out. Her heart was hammering, and she was very tempted to say *No, I'm not OK!* But she didn't. She just said, 'Fine Mrs Goldstein. It's just Sorcha's brother. You can go back inside.'

'All right, dear.'

Mrs Goldstein's door closed and Tiarnan said drily, 'Security system? Together with your knitting needles, I'd say you and Mrs Goldstein could pack quite a punch.'

For some reason Tiarnan's comment hurt Kate terribly. She bit her lip and tried to swallow past the huge lump in her throat. 'What do you want Tiarnan? I'm busy.' She knew she sounded choked and could see Tiarnan's eyes flash in response.

All of a sudden he looked incredibly weary, and Kate could see lines on his face that hadn't been there before. His eyes looked a little bloodshot. Even so, he was still absolutely gorgeous, and she firmed her resolve. Thankfully her composure seemed to come back slightly.

'Kate, can I come in?'

'I'd prefer if you didn't.'

'Please.'

Her composure threatened to crack again, and Kate felt the weight of inevitability fall around her like a cloak. She was pregnant, and she had to tell him sooner or later. In truth, she was terrified of facing this on her own.

Eventually she stood back and held the door open.

Tiarnan walked in, past her, and Kate had to grip the doorknob tight again and close her eyes momentarily as his scent washed over her.

When she'd gathered herself enough after closing the door, she turned to face him. He had taken off his long dark overcoat and she saw that he was wearing a dark sweater and jeans that moulded lovingly to his long legs and hard thigh muscles.

Immediately her belly felt quivery. She felt weak, and moved jerkily to sit on the couch, very aware of his eyes on her.

Kate was as prickly as a porcupine. Tiarnan's eyes drank her in hungrily as she sat down. Her hair was tied back in a high haphazard knot and he longed to undo it. She still looked unbelievably pale, making concern spike through him again. And she looked different, somehow. Even though her cardigan and sweatpants hid her body, he remembered the feel of her slamming into him the previous evening. Every curve and contour.

He felt himself stir to life and cursed. Now was not the time. He had to hold it together—but he couldn't help reacting like a sex-starved teenager. She looked somehow more bountiful, and despite her paleness, more beautiful than he'd ever seen her. It shone right out of her, just as he'd noticed in the ballroom.

'Tiarnan, what is it you want?'

Her husky voice caught him and his eyes met hers. He'd been ogling her like a teenager.

Where to start? Uncharacteristically stuck for words, feeling all at sea and more terrified than he could ever remember feeling, Tiarnan paced up and down, running a hand through his hair. How did he come out and say it? He wanted her—he wanted *it*—he wanted everything. For the first time in his life.

Kate watched Tiarnan pace and saw the look of torture on his face. For the first time she had the awful abject fear that this had nothing to do with *them*. Something else must have happened. She stood, and he stopped pacing and looked at her. She almost couldn't frame the words she was so scared.

'What is it? Is it Rosie? Did something happen? Is it Sorcha or Romain?'

He looked completely nonplussed for a moment, and then comprehension dawned. Kate realised she must have looked terrified, because he was beside her in an instant and sitting her back down, coming with her to sit on the couch.

He shook his head quickly. 'No, nothing's happened to anyone. They're all safe. I'm sorry, Kate, I didn't mean to scare you.'

Relief flooded her—along with the scary realisation that Tiarnan was too close and touching her. She moved back to the corner of the couch. He let go.

She kept silent, but inwardly she was screaming at him to just tell her what he wanted and then leave. She'd even forgotten about telling him of her pregnancy.

Finally he spoke, and it sounded as if it was being torn out of him. 'Kate, I want you.'

Her stomach plummeted. She stood up and moved away, crossing her arms. When would this torture end? She turned to face him. 'Tiarnan, I've told you. I can't do this. I know you want me.' Bitterness laced her voice. 'And you know I want you. But I'm not going there.'

A vivid memory of that woman's face last night outside the restaurant came back into Kate's mind's eye like poison seeping into a wound. Acrid jealousy burned bright within her. 'I'm sure that woman you were with last night can give you what you need.'

Tiarnan stood, and the pain on his face was stark. His hand slashed the air in a gesture of absolute rejection.

'Kate, I couldn't even remember that woman's name after bumping into you—and in truth I was hard pressed to remember it at all. That was my pathetic attempt to try and get back to what I knew, to pretend that you don't exist. To try and block out the fact that I haven't been able to stop thinking about you for a second, the fact that it's taken me weeks of torture to finally realise that I can't live without you. And to block out the fact that I've been haunted with images of you meeting someone else, falling in love with someone else, making love to someone else. Having babies with someone else.'

His eyes burned so intensely blue they held Kate in absolute thrall, unable to move or speak.

His voice sounded rough. 'I wanted to follow you home straight away last night, but I forced myself to wait. I knew that I had to come to you and make you believe what I said— believe that I wasn't just saying it to get you into bed. I was going to be calm, rational, but it's the last thing I feel now. I need *you,* Kate. I don't just want you. *I love you.* And I'm terrified that you won't give me a chance to try and prove to you how much I love you. I'm terrified it might be too late for you to give me a chance to try and make you happy, because I know you want to find someone else. You deserve someone who isn't tainted with mistakes from the past, with an already grown daughter…but I'm selfish, and I don't want you to be with someone else. I want you to be with *me.* For ever.'

Tiarnan's words seem to hang suspended in the air for a long time. Kate didn't know if she was breathing, and then she felt something in her belly quiver. Even though she knew it couldn't be the baby yet, it seemed to inject the life force back into her system.

All the pent-up emotion she'd been keeping down and suppressing for so long seemed to rush up. The fact that she'd all but bared her soul to *him* and yet he'd let her walk away. The torture she'd been going through. She took a jerky step towards Tiarnan, tears prickling, and was so utterly confused and overwhelmed that she hit him ineffectually on his chest, lashing out at the pain he'd caused her. He stood there and let her hit him again, and that made her even more upset. Because even now she couldn't bear to hurt him.

Tears blurred her vision completely and made her voice thick. 'How can you just come in here and say those things? *How?* It's not possible. You can't do this to me, Tiarnan. You can't just walk in and offer me everything I've ever wanted and dreamt of for ever like it's the easiest thing in the world. I've spent a long time getting over you. I don't need you. I've tried so hard to forget you. But now you're here, and you're saying…you're saying…'

She put her hands to her face in turmoil and despair, sobbing her heart out. She sobbed even harder when she felt strong arms wrap around her and pull her close, holding her so tight that somewhere a spark of hope ignited—and the very scary thought that perhaps she wasn't dreaming this. That maybe he had actually said those things and meant them.

Kate had never felt so exposed and raw and emotional in her life. Eventually the sobbing stopped, and she felt her hands being gently pulled away from her face. She was too weak and limp to do anything but look into Tiarnan's eyes, uncaring of how awful she must look. His eyes were full of concern, and something else she'd never seen. *Love.* Tears blurred her vision again.

With the utmost tenderness he cupped her jaw and wiped the tears as they fell with his thumbs.

He sounded tortured. 'Katie, sweetheart. Please don't cry. I'm so sorry for making you cry. I don't ever want to be the cause of making you cry again.' He went very still, and tipped up her chin so she'd look him in the eye. 'I can't bear to see you so upset. If you want me to leave, to walk away, then I'll leave right now.'

She could see the stoic resolve in his eyes. His jaw was clenched, as if to ward off a blow, and a muscle twitched. Kate wiped the back of her hand across her cheek, unaware of the heart-achingly vulnerable image she portrayed. She shook her head and then said softly, shakily, 'If I was stronger I'd make you walk away, so you know what it feels like... But the truth is I'm not that strong. I don't want you to go anywhere. I don't want you to leave my sight ever again.'

Tiarnan put his hands on her upper arms and Kate could feel them shaking. 'Kate, are you saying...? Will you let me try and make you happy?'

Kate finally felt a sense of peace wash through her, diminishing the pain, and with it came trust that this was real. She couldn't keep back a wobbly smile. She put up a hand and touched his jaw. 'Tiarnan, much as I hate to admit this to a man of your supreme confidence, unfortunately you're the only person on this earth who has the power to make me happy. I need *you* so much. I think I've loved you for ever.'

With an unusual lack of grace Tiarnan pulled Kate into him again, then took her face in his hands and kissed her with small feverish kisses saying, *'Thank you...thank you...'* over and over again.

Kate finally stopped him and took *his* face in *her* hands, pressed a long lingering kiss to his mouth. Desire swept up around them, all consuming. Tiarnan's hands roved hungrily over her form, down her back, her hips, her bottom, pulling her in close.

She felt her belly press against him, and had to gasp at the painfully exquisite sensation when he cupped one throbbing and too-sensitive breast. Immediately he pulled back, concern etched on his face.

'What is it?'

Sudden trepidation trickled through Kate. *The pregnancy.* She searched his eyes, terrified that telling him would burst this bubble. But she had to tell him and deal with his response— no matter what it would be.

She pulled back and his hands fell. But she took hold of them tightly.

'When I bumped into you last night I'd just been to see the doctor. That's why I was so distracted…'

Immediately tension came into Tiarnan's body. She'd been so pale. Her cheeks were flushed now, but it could be a fever. 'What is it? Are you OK? Is something wrong?'

She shook her head and said quickly, 'No, nothing's wrong. Everything is fine.'

She smiled shyly then, and all Tiarnan could see was tousled strands of hair falling around her face, her lips plump from his kisses. He wanted to kiss her again so badly, to hold her tight and never wake up from this moment.

He squeezed her hands. 'What is it, Kate?'

She bit her lip and looked down for a moment. Even before she spoke a trickling of awareness came into his body and his consciousness. He recalled how hard her belly had felt just now, how her breasts had felt bigger, more voluptuous. They were obviously sensitive. An incredible joy started to bubble through him even as she looked up and said the words, with naked vulnerability on her face.

'I'm pregnant, Tiarnan. I found out last night. Nearly ten weeks. It must have happened that first night in Martinique…'

Tiarnan could see her start to become nervous.

'I know I said it would be OK—and I really thought it would. It's entirely my fault.'

He immediately shook his head. Anything to stop her talking. He put a finger to her mouth, watched her eyes widen.

'Stop. It's OK. I know what you're thinking, and what you're scared of: that I'll think it's Stella Rios all over again?'

She nodded her head slowly.

'That it's too soon and I might not be ready for this news when we haven't even discussed it?'

She nodded again, her eyes huge and intensely blue.

'Well, don't be. I was halfway to guessing the minute you mentioned the doctor but said you were OK.'

Tiarnan led Kate over to the couch and sat down, pulling her onto his lap. He lifted a hand and kissed it, and then covered her belly with their joined hands, looked into her eyes. 'I never imagined a day when I would be feeling this way about anyone. I'm so in love with you the only time I feel normal or rational or sane is when I can see you and touch you. I've never felt that way about anyone—not even Stella. Never Stella. My association with her was always about the baby, about my responsibility to an unborn child. Stella and I never even consummated the marriage.' He quirked a smile. 'I used her pregnancy as an excuse to hide the fact that I didn't desire her any more. For some reason a blonde-haired blue-eyed witch I'd just kissed kept distracting me.'

His smile faded. 'I should never have rejected you so cruelly that night. The truth is that you'd shocked me out of every arrogant and complacent bone in my body. The desire I felt for you that night was urgent enough that if I hadn't realised how inexperienced you were and remembered *who* you were I would have made love to you there and then, like a randy teenager. I lashed out at that. And then, when you were so cool and blasé, I felt stupidly insulted that you weren't bothered.'

Kate felt pure joy rip through her at his words, at the acknowledgement that it had meant something more for him too. She saw the regret in his eyes, on his face, and smoothed the back of her hand across his cheek. 'We were both young—I was far too young.' She smiled ruefully. 'I don't think I would have been able to handle an experience so intense. And perhaps it's as simple as the fact that Rosie needed you. She wouldn't be in your life now if it hadn't been for Stella.'

Tiarnan felt subtle tension snake into Kate's body and her eyes clouded. He took her hand again. 'What is it? You're closing up on me.'

She shrugged and avoided his eyes. 'It's just that you've only just developed these feelings for me, and you never wanted more children, and I'm just scared… You changed so quickly on Martinique. It scared me how easy you found it to think the worst…'

He pulled her face back to his, forcing her to meet his intense gaze. 'It was easy because I'd never let another woman in so close before. For the first time since Rosie was born I put my needs first and assured myself that Rosie would be OK. When I saw the evidence of her trust in you I panicked. I was terrified I'd lost all sense of judgement and was about to let another woman take advantage of her. I didn't stop to think.'

Kate looked at him, searching as if to see whether she could trust him, and finally said, 'I believe you. I can see how it might have looked… But are you sure you're ready for a baby? You've always—'

He put a finger over her mouth, stopping her words. 'Kate, I've never wanted children again *with anyone else*. But now— with you.' He shrugged with endearing vulnerability. 'I feel like I've been given a gift. A chance to experience something I denied myself for a long time. My background and Stella Rios poisoned my attitudes. You've healed that. These feelings have been brewing for a long, long time. Seeing your desire at the christening that day was merely the catalyst. I've been aware of you all these years, even though I might have denied it to myself. I kept you strictly out of bounds. But you intrigued me with your studied indifference and your coolness. It was just a matter of time before I would have been unable to fight the urge to discover why I couldn't stop thinking about you. I've never felt that same desire for another woman until the moment we kissed again.'

Kate blushed furiously, and Tiarnan tenderly caressed her cheek and said wonderingly, 'Even now you can blush.'

She was still serious for a moment. 'What about Rosie? I mean, does she know about this?'

He nodded, smiling. 'It's one of the two things I did last night, while I tried to restrain myself from coming over here. I told Rosie I was going to come and ask you to marry me, and after she stopped squealing she said, "Does this mean you'll go back to normal now and stop being so crabby?" I assured that I would as long as you said yes, so she's been praying all night that you would say yes.'

He got serious then. 'She cares for you, Kate, and even more importantly she obviously trusts you enough to confide in you. You've already been more of a mother to her than her own mother has been her whole life. She has the picture you sent her in a frame by her bed. A picture I'm extremely jealous of, I might add.'

Kate flushed with pleasure and buried her head against his neck for a moment, hugging him tight. Relief and joy flooded her, because she knew she would never have been happy taking up such a big role in Tiarnan's life unless Rosie was happy too.

She pulled back and pressed a lingering kiss to Tiarnan's mouth. 'You can tell Rosie I said yes. What was the other thing you had to do?'

His eyes flashed in response to her yes, and his hands tightened around her. 'I had to ask Sorcha for her blessing, of course. She told me that if I hurt a hair on your head she'd break my legs—or words to that effect.'

'Great,' Kate grumbled good-naturedly. 'Everyone knew about this before me.'

He looked at her sheepishly. 'There's something else I haven't been able to get out of my mind. You're going to think this sounds crazy, but bumping into you last night made me think of it again. A few years ago I bumped into a girl outside that same restaurant—'

Kate groaned and buried her face in her hands. She mumbled from behind them, 'In a French maid's outfit?'

Tiarnan took down her hands and looked at her, shocked. 'That *was* you?'

She nodded and smiled. 'It was a hen night. I ran away. I was so mortified.'

He shook his head and laughed out loud, head thrown back. 'I thought I was going mad—turned on by some anonymous girl in a tarty costume. Do you realise that after that night I couldn't look at another woman for weeks…months? And at night all I could dream about was you, and wonder what the hell was going on?'

Kate smiled. 'Good! I'm glad I tortured you a little too. It's not entirely fair that I had to endure hearing about your endless parade of women down the years—'

Tiarnan suddenly flipped them, so that Kate lay on the couch underneath him. He undid her hair until it flowed out around her head. He ran a hand over her burgeoning breasts, causing her breath to catch, and down to her belly, caressing the growing mound.

Kate put her hand over his and felt the exquisite quickening of desire that only this man could engender. She pulled his head down and said throatily, 'First, before I kiss you all over your body to within an inch of your life, Tiarnan Quinn, I have to tell you something else.'

Tiarnan had already started kissing her, pulling her top up.

Kate stopped him and looked at him mock sternly. '*Wait.*'

She smiled, then brought his hand back to her now bare belly and looked at him with shining eyes. 'How do you feel about twins?'

He stopped and looked down at her, eyes widening in wonder. 'Seriously?'

Kate nodded. His hand tightened on her belly. An unmis-

takably proprietorial gleam lit his intense gaze, making Kate
rejoice inwardly.

He growled softly. 'Tell me how much it's going to cost to
buy you out of every job contract and campaign you're booked
for—because you and our babies are mine now, and I'm not
letting another person have the right to touch you or photograph
you without my say-so.'

Kate smiled and revelled in his innate possessiveness. She
shifted easily under him, feeling the heavy weight of his arousal
pressing against his jeans. She moved sinuously. Colour stained
his cheeks.

'Kate,' he said warningly.

She made a quick calculation and said a round figure. He
paled slightly under his tan, but didn't miss a beat. 'I paid a
fraction of that just to kiss you, so I figure it's worth it to marry
you, to be the father of your children and live happily ever after.'

'Sounds good to me.' Kate smiled, and pulled him back
down to where she wanted him for ever—in her arms.

● EPILOGUE

Two and a half years later, Martinique

KATE stood in the dim light and looked lovingly at the two small sprawled forms in the big double bed, protected by a muslin net hanging from above. Dark-haired Iris was on her back, thumb stuck firmly in her mouth and sucking periodically. Blonde-haired Nell was on her front, arms outstretched, her head resting on one chubby cheek and looking angelic. Kate smiled. She'd been anything but angelic a few hours ago.

Pure joy rose up within her, and she had to press a hand to her chest to try and contain it. And then she felt a big solid presence behind her, strong arms wrap around her waist. She leant back into the familiar embrace and smiled wider when she felt firm lips press a hot kiss to her neck.

They were in the room that had been hers the first time she'd come to Martinique. Now it was a nursery for the girls. She heard Tiarnan whisper close to her ear, 'We'll have to put bars around the room. I caught Nell making a near-successful bid for freedom earlier.'

Kate stifled a giggle at the image.

Tiarnan took her hand to lead her out and back to their own room along the balcony. He was in nothing but boxer shorts, and Kate's eyes ran over him appreciatively. Tiarnan caught her looking. He stopped and pulled her into his arms.

'Why, Mrs Quinn,' he said mock seriously, 'I think I'm feeling a little violated by your very explicit look.'

Kate leant into him luxuriously, loving the feel of his body, and especially the way it was reacting. She wrapped her arms around him and pressed a kiss to his neck. 'I'm very sorry, Mr Quinn. I know how sensitive you are.'

He groaned softly when he felt her move her hips, bringing the apex of her legs into close contact with his rapidly hardening arousal.

Kate looked at him, revelling in the intimate moment. Revelling in the bliss to come and the bliss she felt every day. She took his hand to lead him into their bedroom.

He asked on the way, 'What was wrong with Rosie earlier? Apparently I "wouldn't understand".'

Kate looked back and smiled. 'It's nothing, really—just girlie issues. She likes one of Zoe's cousins, but he likes someone else…'

Tiarnan groaned, and said with feeling, 'I knew there was a reason I married you. I could never deal with all this puberty stuff.'

Kate hit his arm playfully and said something—but it was indistinct as they disappeared into the bedroom, and then everything faded into the beautifully warm and fragrant tropical darkness.

millsandboon.co.uk Community

Join Us!

The Community is the perfect place to meet and chat to
kindred spirits who love books and reading as much as
you do, but it's also the place to:

- **Get the inside scoop from authors about their latest books**
- **Learn how to write a romance book with advice from our editors**
- **Help us to continue publishing the best in women's fiction**
- **Share your thoughts on the books we publish**
- **Befriend other users**

Forums: Interact with each other as well as authors, editors and a whole host of other users worldwide.

Blogs: Every registered community member has their own blog to tell the world what they're up to and what's on their mind.

Book Challenge: We're aiming to read 5,000 books and have joined forces with The Reading Agency in our inaugural Book Challenge.

Profile Page: Showcase yourself and keep a record of your recent community activity.

Social Networking: We've added buttons at the end of every post to share via digg, Facebook, Google, Yahoo, technorati and de.licio.us.

www.millsandboon.co.uk

2 FREE BOOKS
AND A SURPRISE GIFT

We would like to take this opportunity to thank you for reading this Mills & Boon® book by offering you the chance to take TWO more specially selected books from the Modern™ series absolutely FREE! We're also making this offer to introduce you to the benefits of the Mills & Boon® Book Club™—

- **FREE home delivery**
- **FREE gifts and competitions**
- **FREE monthly Newsletter**
- **Exclusive Mills & Boon Book Club offers**
- **Books available before they're in the shops**

Accepting these FREE books and gift places you under no obligation to buy, you may cancel at any time, even after receiving your free books. Simply complete your details below and return the entire page to the address below. You don't even need a stamp!

YES Please send me 2 free Modern books and a surprise gift. I understand that unless you hear from me, I will receive 4 superb new books every month for just £3.19 each, postage and packing free. I am under no obligation to purchase any books and may cancel my subscription at any time. The free books and gift will be mine to keep in any case.

Ms/Mrs/Miss/Mr _____   Initials _____

Surname _____

Address _____

_____   Postcode _____

Send this whole page to: Mills & Boon Book Club, Free Book Offer, FREEPOST NAT 10298, Richmond, TW9 1BR

Offer valid in UK only and is not available to current Mills & Boon Book Club subscribers to this series. Overseas and Eire please write for details. We reserve the right to refuse an application and applicants must be aged 18 years or over. Only one application per household. Terms and prices subject to change without notice. Offer expires 31st December 2009. As a result of this application, you may receive offers from Harlequin Mills & Boon and other carefully selected companies. If you would prefer not to share in this opportunity please write to The Data Manager, PO Box 676, Richmond, TW9 1WU.

Mills & Boon® is a registered trademark owned by Harlequin Mills & Boon Limited.
Modern™ is being used as a trademark. The Mills & Boon® Book Club™ is being used as a trademark.